Keepsake

KEEPSAKE

First published in 2017 by
Little Island Books
7 Kenilworth Park
Dublin 6W
Ireland

ISBN: 978-1-910411-57-5

A British Library Cataloguing in Publication record for this book is available from the British Library.

Cover illustration by Olivia Golden
Insides designed and typeset by www.redrattledesign.com

Printed in Poland by Drukarnia Skleniarz

Little Island receives financial assistance from
The Arts Council/An Chomhairle Ealaíon and the Arts Council of Northern Ireland

10 9 8 7 6 5 4 3 2 1

Keepsake

PAULA LEYDEN

Little
Island

For Tom

A Soft Nose

Ella stood on the wet grass, a small frown on her face. She peered through the rails then put one foot onto the bottom rung of the gate and pulled herself up to get a better view. She smiled. He was there, right down in the bottom corner of the field next to the old hawthorn tree, rubbing his neck vigorously against the rough bark. She called out, quietly so that no-one but him could hear her, but he didn't look up. She called again, a little louder, looking over her shoulder to make sure no-one was listening. This time he heard. She watched as he raised his head and looked straight at her, his ears facing forward. Alert. Ready. She kept perfectly still, balancing on the gate. She didn't want to scare him.

He took a step forward, then stopped. As she knew he would. He was shy. But she would be patient. She had all the time in the world.

On the first day he had run from her and she'd watched as he jumped across the small ditch then stopped and turned around. To watch her from a safe distance. Ella knew about that. 'Fight or flight' they called it. It was instinct. Some animals would fight when they were scared; others would run away. Horses definitely ran away. It protected them from ancient predators, from the sleek snow leopards who had prowled the steppes all those thousands of years ago, taut bodies ready to spring.

This beautiful creature in front of her remembered them, those wild cats. It was a memory handed down over the centuries. When his time came he too would pass it on to those who came after him.

She waited and she watched, oblivious to the damp chill in the air, oblivious to everything except him.

His breath formed small white clouds in the cool air as he shook his head and the breeze lifted his long mane. She breathed in. Today she knew he would come closer. He'd just been making sure the last time. Testing her. She would pass the test and he would remember that too. She smiled, wondering whether he could feel her smiling, see her happiness. Perhaps he could.

Suddenly, without warning, he started trotting. He moved in a wide circle, his neck arched and his tail held high. High-stepping, he circled the field, pretending to ignore her. As he passed her, just metres away from the gate, he dropped his neck down and whinnied. A sound sweeter than any she had ever heard. A small lump formed in her throat. He was talking to her; he knew she loved him.

He slowed down on his third circle and then came to a stop right in front of her. She didn't move. He took a step towards her, then another, till his beautiful black face was right next to hers. She felt the warm breath of him breathed through his nostrils. She bent towards him and rubbed her head gently against his nose. He did not move.

When she raised her head he stepped back. Not scared, he just had other things to be doing. He returned to the old hawthorn and stopped, leaning in to resume his scratching. As if nothing had interrupted him. But she knew better. She would go back across the fields, her secret held close to her heart. Today, on Monday the seventeenth of May, he had introduced himself to her.

Black Molly and Cloudy Thoughts

Ella's granny, Orla Mackey, had three rules in her home – all of them designed for when Ella came to stay with her:

Rule 1 No sleeping past eight in the morning

Rule 2 There is no magic cleaning fairy living in this house.

Rule 3 Your phone goes to sleep when you go to bed – and its bed is downstairs in the kitchen. It eats somewhere else as well, never at the table.

The rest was up to Ella. Her granny, within reason, did not mind what she did during the day, apart from the unspoken fourth rule – the dogs, Grouse, Old Greg and Annie, won't walk themselves. This suited Ella because, as long as she had them with her, her granny asked no questions. Which is why she was here, standing outside Delaney's field talking to a wondrous horse. As she turned to walk home she wondered about him. About why he was alone in the field. She'd never seen anyone with him, horse nor human. It was as if he'd appeared from nowhere. It was also strange that he was the same colour as Black Molly, the mare that had lived on the farm when her granny was the same age as Ella was now.

Last night her granny had told her one of her stories about Black Molly. Each time she told her a story Ella recorded it on her phone and then typed it up into a file called 'Granny's Stories'. Just because.

It was a bright June night, close to the summer solstice, and Black Molly was pacing around her field. Her huge belly was swaying from side to side. I knew she was ready to foal. My mam and dad, your great grandparents, couldn't persuade me to go to bed. I was your age, Ella, eleven years old exactly. I knew all the signs. Small drops of milk were dripping from her teats, she was ready. Eventually after begging and pleading with them they agreed. I could be on foal watch but I had to promise to wake them if she started.

I couldn't watch her from where she could see me or she might not foal. No mare likes to be watched and I don't really blame them, so I made a small hideout for myself in the shed that looked out onto the paddock. I took a mug of tea with me and a cheese sandwich and settled in for a long night. It was past eleven o clock when it started to get dark and the moon rose. Black Molly had started to sweat and I knew she was very close.

I should have called for help, I'd promised them I would, but I didn't want to leave in case I missed it. I suppose I wanted to be the first human to see the little foal.

And I was. But not in the way I'd thought. I fell asleep, Ella. Right there in the shed on the blanket I'd put over the straw to stop my legs itching. Fast asleep. I only woke up when I heard Black Molly whinnying just next to the shed. I opened my eyes and there she was. With wobbly, skinny, long-legged Giant by her side. I've never, not in all my years, woken up to a more beautiful sight than that.

He was dark like the night but around his eyes were little rings of white. He looked just like a clown. I knew then that the colour of his clown eyes would be the colour he'd be when he grew up.

I gave Black Molly the treats I had for her, a crunchy red apple and one carrot, and put my hand through the gate so Giant could sniff me. His soft little nose twitching. Then I called my parents. It was lucky everything was all right; otherwise they would have been very cross. But they weren't, so it all worked out, and little Giant had arrived.

It was hard for Ella to imagine her granny with parents but it wasn't hard to imagine her as a little girl. She wasn't sure why that was but it was true. And she knew why her granny hadn't called her parents on the night Giant was born. There are some things you want to keep to yourself just for a bit. It was the same with the horse in Delaney's field. If she told no-one then it was only her and him without the rest of the world looking in. She knew her granny wasn't exactly the rest of the world, and eventually she would tell her granny (if only because she was the hardest person in the world to keep a secret from), but right now she liked having him as her secret.

She loved her granny now. It wasn't always like that because she was hard to get used to. Ella could tell the exact moment that she had started loving her granny, because it was at the end of one of her stories. Quite often her granny would end by saying, 'so that's it' and that day, the twenty-fifth of August last year just before she had to go back to school, just after she ended her story with these exact words, it happened. She saw her granny's thoughts. That's when she knew.

Ella's biggest secret was that she could sometimes see what was going on in the minds of people she loved. Not always. It was as if she got tiny glimpses into their heads with no warning whatsoever. Sometimes she saw pictures. Not often. Other times she just sensed feelings. Especially when the person was trying to hide them. Happiness. Sadness. Love. Anger. Laughter. Tears. The only things she never saw were words. It would be hard to explain this thing to anyone who didn't know, so she didn't try.

With her dad the thoughts and feelings were easier to make out, orderly and square, straight edges. Much tidier than he was himself. But with her granny from that first day the thoughts were like little puffs of smoke, small cloudy pictures. Floating softly above her head. Cluttered thoughts that were not always easy to see because they bumped into one another, curled around each other and then sometimes unfurled. It was only when they did that that she could see them properly.

At night now she sometimes dreamed about her dad's thoughts because she could no longer see them. For the simple reason that she could no longer see him. Each night he'd text her from Dubbo, a small town in Australia where he'd been living for the past three years:

Night, sweetie-pie,
sweet dreams,
see you soon.

Her granny said that that was a lot of sweetness for a mining man, but she laughed when she said it. Ella only wondered how soon soon was, but she treasured the texts. Sometimes he'd send her a fact about Australia or a picture of something like a kookaburra bird. She'd imagine the texts travelling around the world to her, small wordy glow-worms. Seventeen thousand and fifty-one kilometres was the distance between Dubbo and Carrigcapall. A long way to fly. Hopefully one of these days he'd come back. She missed him more than she could even think about.

At the start of this summer she'd decided to ask her granny whether she could move to the farm to live with her until her dad got back. It wasn't that Ella didn't love her mum. She did. In some sort of a way. But it got lonely in Dublin because Damien 'you can call me Dad' Conway was always around and he was loud and irritating so Ella just stayed in her room after school. She knew two things about him: she would never call him Dad and his thoughts were invisible to her. Which was how she wanted it.

She hadn't broached the subject yet about staying on the farm but today she just might; it seemed like the right time. She wanted to be here, where her dad had grown up and where there was at least the possibility that one day she could have a horse all of her own.

The Locked Door

When Ella came in after her walk she headed straight for the Aga. Her granny wasn't in the kitchen. Not that Ella could see anyway. And that wasn't because the kitchen was huge, it was just very full. It always seemed to Ella that it was a little bit like her granny's head. Most things in it were hung from the ceiling: pots and pans, washing, onions, baskets, jugs, mugs, coats and teapots. The things that weren't suspended from the ceiling were in presses that were fit to burst. Her granny's explanation was that many people had lived in this house before her and each one of them had left just a little bit of themselves behind.

Ella called out to her. The kettle was on top of the Aga so she had to be around.

'That was a long walk,' her granny replied, from somewhere.

'Where are you?' Ella said.

'In the pantry,' her granny said, as if that was the most normal place in the world to be.

Ella turned her head and, sure enough, the door into the

room her granny called the pantry was unlocked, slightly ajar. Ever since Ella had been coming here to visit, that door had been locked. To keep the cold out was what her granny always said, because that room was too close to the outside. Her dad had told her that it wasn't any closer to the outside than the rest of the house; it was just that there was something about the room that upset her but he wasn't sure what it was.

Ella walked slowly towards the door. 'I'm coming in,' she said a little shakily. At that precise moment her granny opened the door and stepped through, closing it and then locking it very firmly behind her.

'No need,' she said, a small smile on her face, 'and where were you?'

Ella looked at her. The grey cloud above her head did not look very smiley.

'Walking,' she replied, surprised by the question.

Her granny stared at her with her head tilted to one side. 'Hmmmmm. Did you see anything interesting on the walk?'

Unbidden images of the horse came into her head and she tried to shake them away. 'Just the usual,' she said, which was a not-saying-exactly-what-you-mean kind of a truth.

Her granny smiled. 'The usual is always good.'

'Granny,' Ella said, thinking now was as good a time as any, 'I've been thinking.'

Her granny turned to take the kettle off and stoke up the fire in the Aga. 'Yes?'

'Well, you know how I come here for the summer and on weekends and in the holidays and all that?'

'I do.'

'Wouldn't it be easier if I just stayed here, you know, most of the time? I could walk the dogs and we wouldn't waste all that money on the bus and then I could visit Mum sometimes but she won't be lonely because she has Damien and I know the dogs don't like it when I leave and I think you're a bit old to be living by yourself and then I'll be here when dad comes back.' Ella drew breath. 'And, I can go to school here, it won't be as crowded.' She stopped, looking at her granny who was still standing with her back to her. At least the sad cloud above her head had paled a little, which was a good sign.

'A bit old?' she asked.

'Well, not very old just older than me, that's all, not old like – Mr Murphy or something.' As Mr Murphy was the oldest man anyone had ever met that wasn't much consolation.

'And you'd miss Dublin, I think.'

'No I wouldn't. Sometimes I can't breathe properly in Dublin and all the noise makes my head hurt.' This was a slight exaggeration but sometimes you needed to exaggerate just to get your point across.

'And what about Mum?' her granny said, finally turning round to look at Ella.

Ella looked down at the floor. 'Well, yes, she'll miss me, but she says whatever makes me happy.' Which she did but not always in the happiest kind of voice. 'And she can come here to visit.'

'And you'll miss her.'

'I know. But ... Dad would like it if I was here.'

'I'll think about it. We've got all summer, but I promise I'll think about it,' her granny said. It was her way of ending the conversation.

Ella knew to say nothing more.

Truth and Magpies

The next morning as Ella headed out for her walk, her granny called her back.

'Where are you walking today?' she asked. For the first time ever.

Ella scrambled around in her head for an answer that wouldn't be a lie. 'Just around the place, you know, where I usually go.'

Her granny looked at her. 'No, I suppose I don't know, petal. I'm not even sure why I've never asked you. Perhaps because you remind me so much of your dad and I never asked him. But I mostly knew where he was because he was helping out in the fields, but there's nothing much left to help out with now. So?'

'Well,' Ella began, wondering why she hadn't just told her in the first place, 'I go through the humpy bumpy field, then round the twelve-acre field then into the river field but I don't cross the river and through the triangle field and then into the rath field and then I cross into the tower field and I end up in Roches' field because they don't mind and there are no cows in it at the moment because they grazed it flat and then ... and then sometimes I pass Delaney's field, the one next to the field that's next to the road. And there's a horse in it.'

Her granny smiled. 'A horse?' A question that sounded as if she had known all along that this would be where Ella would end up eventually.

'Yes, Granny, he's black and I was wondering if he might be one of Black Molly's descendants, he's the exact colour you described, and his mane is longer than my hair and I think he's getting to know me, last time he definitely recognised me, he whinnied and it almost sounded like he was calling me or something. I was thinking that that field is quite small and I've never seen anyone in there with him so maybe no-one owns him and he might like to come and live in the twelve-acre field because now you don't have anything in it and you're not using it so it might as well be used and I think Black Molly would be really pleased if she could see that he's there because isn't that the field you buried her in?' Ella drew breath.

'It is that field,' her granny said, 'but I'm sure someone owns this horse, Ella. There can't be a horse in a field with a closed gate that no-one owns, unless you think he jumped in there? And you're not supposed to be walking on the road, you know that?'

'I know, I never go on the road, I go to the other side of the field. Where the gate is. Maybe you'd like to come and see him with me one day and maybe ... maybe we can talk about me learning to ride. Again. I know you don't think it's a good idea, you said I'm too young, but I'm eleven now.'

Suddenly a thought unfurled above her granny's head and Black Molly appeared, tall and graceful, cantering around. Looking just as she did in the photos of her. Except it seemed as though someone was on her back. But the picture came and went so quickly that Ella might have been imagining it.

'I know, petal, and eleven is old enough. We will talk about it, just not right now if that's OK?'

Ella nodded, knowing that 'not right now' could mean anything at all. It could mean waiting till next year, as it had been a very, very long time since the last conversation about learning to ride.

'In the meantime don't go into the field. If he's on his own he could be a stallion. Promise me you'll stay outside the gate? And keep the dogs outside the gate as well. Horses are beautiful but you never know what they are going to do. Especially stallions.'

'I know, Granny, I won't go in.'

'Is he well fed?' her granny asked. 'Can you see his ribs?'

Ella shook her head. 'No ribs at all, he's beautiful.'

Her granny laughed. 'Well I can tell you something for nothing: someone owns that horse. He wouldn't be beautiful on the pickings of that field alone. If you want you can take a couple of carrots for him, or an apple, but nothing else. Now on you go and be careful, you promise me? And take that mad magpie hound with you as well as the others, will you, he's quiet round most other creatures so I'm sure a horse won't bother him.'

Ella laughed. Old Greg the collie had arrived on the farm at the start of summer, thin and frightened with a heavy chain around his neck. Ella's granny had started leaving food out for him and slowly he'd come closer and closer. He'd still not agreed to come into the house but they'd made him a comfortable bed in the hay shed and he seemed happy about that. He mostly ignored Grouse and Annie, except when Annie tried to steal his food. The only creatures he didn't ignore were the magpies. From early morning he would patrol the farm searching for them. Then he'd sit at the bottom of whichever tree they were in and bark incessantly. Ella always worried that he'd catch one, until one day she saw him walking down the field with a magpie on his back and two others following him. Waddling along, not a bother in the world, almost like baby ducklings. Secretly Ella wondered whether he was in fact a magpie himself with the power to turn into a collie when it suited him. Maybe when he felt like a rub. Not many people would give a magpie a rub.

'It's not the one way we all go mad,' her granny had said, 'and there are worse ways to go than talking to magpies.'

Which was true, Ella thought, as she called him. Take her mum, for example. Not that she was mad, but Ella would prefer if she wandered around the fields talking to magpies instead of wandering around the apartment talking to Damien.

The Boy and his Horse

As Ella left the house she thought about her mum. She closed her eyes for a moment and her mum's face came into her head. As she was before. When she was still with Ella's dad. Smiling. Not all the time but most of the time. Talkative. Her dad used to put his hand over her mouth sometimes. 'Enough,' he'd say, laughing at her, 'my ears are bleeding from all the chat.' But then that stopped, Ella couldn't even remember when, but the house had become quieter. No-one seemed to talk very much then, apart from Ella who thought if she carried on talking at every opportunity her mum and dad would start again. But it didn't happen. And then one day, the twenty-fourth of September last year it all went completely wrong. Ella remembered that day as if it was yesterday. Dad came into her bedroom in Dublin and sat down on her bed. Heavily. 'I'm going to go away for a bit, petal,' he'd said. He always called her 'petal', just like Granny did. 'To Australia. It won't be for long, it's just to earn some money, then I'll be back. Mum and I ... well, Mum and I need a break from each other.'

Mum hadn't said a lot about it. And then he'd gone. As Ella walked along her well-worn path through the fields she wondered if he would ever come back. She also wondered if he would be the same as he was before. Mum wasn't at all the same, but Ella was used to her now. She shook her head to get rid of her thoughts. Dad used to say to her that if her thoughts became too heavy then she needed to shake her head and throw them off for a while; otherwise her neck would bend with the weight of them. Sometimes it worked. Today it did because she was on her way to see the horse.

When she reached the small field, there he was in his favourite corner. She stood up on the gate and started to call him before she realised that he wasn't alone. She jumped back down off the gate in fright, almost falling in the process. There was a young boy standing next to him and rubbing his neck. Ella quickly ducked behind a piece of corrugated iron propped up next to the gate and called the dogs to her as quietly as she could. She wished, not for the first time, that Annie was as obedient as the others. But she wasn't. She looked at Ella, her ears pricked forward, as if deciding whether or not today would be the day she'd do what she was told. She thought better of it and started racing up and down next to the fence, barking. The young boy looked up and frowned, then whistled very loudly at Annie to call her to him. *Good luck with that,* Ella thought. True to form, Annie ignored him and continued her barking. The boy turned back to the horse and ran his hand down his neck and along his back. Then, in what seemed to Ella like a split second, he lifted himself up and onto the horse's back. He had the halter lead rope in one hand and the horse's long flowing mane in the other.

Ella peeped out from behind the corrugated sheet to get a better view. The horse started moving in exactly the same way he had the day before. Slowly at first in a small circle then widening the circle and lifting his legs up into a graceful high-stepping trot. The young boy sat easily on him and urged him on faster till the horse broke into a gentle canter. As they disappeared behind the bank of hawthorns at the bottom of the paddock, Ella darted out from her hiding place and ran through the gap into the tower field. Far enough away that he wouldn't be able to see her.

She wasn't quite sure why she was hiding. Maybe because she was sure that the boy thought he was alone. And if you think you're alone then you don't really want anyone watching you. In her head the horse hadn't belonged to anyone. Sure, her granny said that was not possible. But he had seemed like a horse that would only do what he had decided to do himself. A horse with no limits. A horse that had spoken to her just one day ago.

She started the long walk back home with her heart just a little sore. She hated seeing the horse with someone else; it changed everything. And they knew each other so well, the horse and the boy, better than she did. Maybe he'd fall off and break his leg and then he'd need someone to look after the horse and she'd be there and then he'd be the one standing at the gate watching them. She shook her head.

Ella, that's an awful thought. And he didn't look like he'd fall off anyway, even with no saddle and no bridle. That's how she'd like to learn to ride. No horrible piece of metal in the horse's mouth, no girth being pulled around his belly. Maybe next time she'd speak to the boy and when she got to know him he might teach her to ride the way he did.

She neared the back gate and smiled as she imagined herself sitting on the horse's strong, firm back. Maybe, after a while, she'd even ask the boy if he'd like to share him with her. She shivered. No, that was too much to think about. But her dad always told her that impossible was just a word, so maybe ...

Magic and Storm

Johnny sat on top of Storm and watched through the branches of the tree as the girl darted away. He frowned. He didn't know her. No-one apart from Delaney ever came near this field, and it was his field so he had good reason to be here. But no-one else, ever. That's why he liked it. No-one to bother him. It was tucked away and couldn't be seen from the road. Storm was safe here.

He leaned forward. 'Still, boy,' he whispered to the restless horse. 'We'll wait till she's gone, then we can move.' Storm was sweating lightly underneath him, twitching the flies away. Johnny thought back to the day Storm had become his. A sad and happy day all bundled into the one. Happy because he got Storm. Sad because Grandma had died.

Before she got sick he'd not thought much about whether she would ever die. Because she was just always there. Always alive. And strong. There seemed to be nothing she couldn't do. And never in a way that let you know she was doing it and wasn't she great. No. She was just always there if you needed anything. And she never looked that old. Maybe because every few weeks when any grey hairs started appearing they would be sent back to where they came from by a tube of black dye. But then she got sick and things were never the same after that.

He pressed his legs against Storm and urged him forward. He wished he could do this every day instead of school. Because his head never hurt when he was out here. No matter if it was raining or cold or even snowing. It didn't matter. Because it was just him and Storm and no-one to hassle him, no-one to make him learn things that were never going to be any use. He didn't mind the maths, it was OK, quick enough to get done, but the reading made his eyes sore. No way of avoiding it, though. If he didn't go to school his mam would be after him even quicker than the teachers. It used to be his grandma – she was in charge of all that. But now it was his mam.

When he reached the gate he leant down and unhooked it, closing it carefully behind him. The sun came out from behind the cloud and shone on Storm's sleek blackness. He was the only black foal that Magic had ever had. The others were all coloured, both before and since. But four years ago she'd had Storm. Not a single splash of white on him anywhere. Not his belly or his face, not even a sock of white. Johnny loved him for that. And loved that although he was a stallion he was as quiet as a pet for him. He was his keepsake of his grandma and he would never be parted from him. He would not let them take him in the same way they'd taken Magic just before Christmas. The thought of that made his head hurt even more than reading did.

As Johnny walked back home after filling up the water trough for Storm, he thought about the girl who'd been watching him. It made him nervous. The last time someone had been watching him like that had been the day before Magic was taken. He turned back. He'd find a way to hide Storm. Just in case.

The field was rough and stony at the start of it but in the space behind the hawthorn tree there was a hidden section. No-one standing at the gate would be able to see a horse in there, even if they were looking for one. The grass was thick, so Storm would be all right for a day or so.

He called Storm, and the horse came towards him. They knew each other so well that Johnny didn't even need to put the lead rope on him; the horse just followed him. Which was handy, because once the horse was safely inside the space, Johnny strung the lead rope across the gap to prevent him escaping. It wasn't perfect but it would do. Then if the girl told anyone about him they wouldn't be able to see him. He took a handful of feed out of his pocket and held it out to him. He loved the feel of Storm's mouth against the palm of his hand. Next he dragged the small trough across the field till he reached the grassy space.

He looked at Storm. Some people would think it was mad that every time he looked into Storm's eyes he thought of his grandma. But it didn't matter. It was just the way it was. And it wasn't as if they were alike. His grandma could be very fierce when she felt like it and he'd never seen

Storm like that. But still her memory was inside Storm and always would be. Just like the memory of his uncle was inside Magic till she was taken by the pound.

Johnny shut his eyes tightly against the image of Magic being pulled into a cattle trailer and taken away. That was the last time he'd seen her.

They Kill Horses There

The next morning when Ella woke up the house was very quiet. No banging or clattering of pots. No dogs barking. No singing. Her granny was one of those people who sang as she worked. Ella used to think that no-one had ever told her that her singing was really out of tune. Not mildly out of tune, just completely tee-totally out of tune. But she soon discovered that everyone had in fact told her but her granny just didn't care. Maybe the same head that sang out of tune was unable to realise it did, no matter how many times it was told. Her dad told her it was probably because Granny only ever heard what she wanted to hear, which Ella thought wasn't quite fair.

But this morning the house was silent. She walked down the stairs, and the creaking of the oak steps sounded much louder than it usually did. She pushed open the kitchen door and it was empty. It was only then she heard faint sounds coming from behind the pantry door.

'Granny?' she said, knocking lightly on the door.

'Yes.'

'Everything OK?'

'Yes.'

Ella stood for a while, hoping something else was about to be said.

Nothing.

'Granny?'

'Yes.'

'Can I come in?'

'No. You get your breakfast and I'll be out in a bit.'

'Where are the dogs?'

'In here with me. We'll be out soon.'

Ella knew there was no point carrying on the conversation, so she went to the press to get the cereal out. When she first started coming to stay here on her own, her granny had emptied out a kitchen press and stuck a notice on it which said 'Ella's Press'. In it were all the things that she knew Ella liked, including Frosties. Which she didn't approve of but knew Ella did so she made an exception for her. 'That's what you are, Ella,' she'd said to her one day, 'an exception, and that's all right.'

It felt quite odd sitting at the kitchen table with no Granny and no dogs, knowing that they were just the other side of the door, but she wasn't allowed in to them. And why were the dogs so quiet? Annie she could understand, she was a whippet and she was either racing around like a mad thing or curled up asleep. But Grouse? Grouse was a springer and anyone who has ever had a springer knows that they are two things – emotional and energetic. Grouse could go on twenty walks a day and still be waiting for you to take him on another. Yet now they were making no sound at all. The only noises coming from inside the room were Granny noises. No singing, just moving stuff around.

Ella, who was not by nature sneaky, crept towards the door and quietly pressed her ear against it. She could hear murmuring in there, Granny murmuring, but it was very hard to make out the words.

'Ella!'

Ella jumped at the sound, which was very loud through the door, and she fell backwards, knocking over the sweeping brush that was standing next to it.

She blushed.

'Yes, Granny. Sorry, Granny. I was just wondering –'

'Stop. Don't tell me. Just eat your breakfast, petal. I'll be out in a minute.'

Ella picked up the broom and sat down again. Mortified.

Within minutes she heard the door opening, and her granny, followed by the dogs, came back into the kitchen. Ella looked at her and breathed a sigh of relief – there were no angry thoughts hovering above her head. If she wasn't mistaken some of the thoughts were laughing.

'Hi, Granny,' she said, as her granny leaned down and kissed the top of her head.

'Hi, petal, for the second time. Although I suppose strictly speaking even though we spoke I didn't see you, so that's not quite the same thing is it?'

Ella shook her head. 'I suppose not,' she said, wondering how she could change the subject.

'Granny? I was thinking we could Skype Dad today.'

'Well, let's see what the time is in Dubbo. It's nine o'clock here so it'll be four o'clock there so he won't be back from work. We'll call in a couple of hours, will we? You could go out for a walk and when you're back the time will be right.'

'OK.'

'Did you see that horse yesterday?'

'I did.' Ella hesitated. She wasn't quite sure why she didn't want to tell her granny about the boy but she knew she didn't. Not yet anyway.

'And?' her granny said, staring at a point just above Ella's head. A familiar sight to Ella, it was the point she stared at above anyone's head whose thoughts she could sometimes see. Could be a coincidence but it did confirm her suspicion that her granny was blessed or cursed with the same ability. Under these circumstances she had to make a quick decision.

'Well, there was a boy there. I think he must be the one who owns him. He was riding the horse.'

Her granny smiled. 'I thought he might have been owned. It would be strange to come across a horse in a field, looking so well, with no owner. And he must be a stallion if he's on his own. You know never to go near a stallion, Ella. They may look peaceful but he doesn't know you. Stallions are unpredictable.'

'I know that, Granny, you've told me that before.'

'It doesn't mean you don't need to listen, does it, petal?'

Ella shook her head.

'I always feel sorry for the stallions being on their own,' her granny said. 'When they were wild they would run in herds together, the stallions, the mares and the foals. Much nicer. Did you talk to the boy?'

Ella shook her head. 'No, Granny. I hid. I don't know why but I didn't want him to see me. Maybe because he looked like he was used to being on his own. You know when someone does something and they don't know they're being watched? He was like that, so I hid and then I ran away.'

Her granny looked at her. 'That's kind, petal, but there probably wasn't a very good hiding place if my memory of Delaney's field is right? So he might have seen you. And maybe he doesn't mind. Next time you could try and talk to him. But never go into the field. Ever. Promise me.'

'I promise. But I don't know if I will talk to him. I'm not as good at talking to people as you are but I'll try. I'll go there now with the dogs – he might be back.'

'Do that, and later I might just have another story for you, one I'd forgotten about. I think you'll like it.' She gave Ella a quick hug. 'Don't forget the apples,' she said as she handed her a bag. 'He'll like those. And be careful!'

'I will.'

'Ella?'

'Yes, Granny?'

'Don't just say "I will" like that. I'm serious. Mind yourself. Think of the size of a horse and the size of you. There's a big difference.'

'I know, Granny. I am very careful, I promise.'

Ella opened the door, and the dogs, needing no invitation, rushed past her. Every time she took them for a walk, they behaved as if this was their first walk ever. Today was no different. She headed out of the gate and into the fields. The grass was still damp from the dew and Grouse already looked like a wet mop. He was never happier than when he was soaked through.

She hoped in one way that the boy was there, but in another that he wasn't and she could have the horse to herself. She slowed down when she reached the field and approached it carefully. When she got to the gate there was nothing there. No horse. No boy. She stood up on the railing of the gate, her eyes moving slowly around the outgrown blackthorn hedges, hoping against hope that if she scanned carefully she'd see a sign of him. Maybe he'd gone too deep into the ditch to try to get at the sweet bark of the young sally trees and had got trapped in there. Hurt himself. There was absolutely no sign of him. The boy must have seen her and taken the horse away. That was all. She'd never see him again.

When she slowly stepped down from the gate, disappointment burning her eyes, she thought she saw a slight movement. Behind the hawthorn trees in the far corner. Just a small one. Could have been the wind. Then she heard it. A low whinny. He was here; the boy hadn't taken him. She smiled, then she heard it again. He sounded different. Perhaps he was in trouble. Her heart started pounding and, without thinking, she climbed over the gate and started running down towards the clump of trees, closely followed by Grouse and Annie. Old Greg stayed sitting behind the gate. When she reached the trees she saw him. He was standing there almost as if he was expecting her. Strung between two of the trees was a faded red rope, closing the gap into the space. She stood still. She'd never been this close to him without a gate between them. She suddenly remembered her granny's warning that stallions could be unpredictable and here she was with only a rope between her and him.

She looked at him and he looked straight back at her, making no move to come closer. She reached into the bag and pulled out an apple and bit a large chunk out of it, then put it flat on the palm of her hand. Slowly she reached out to him. He sniffed the apple then very gently lifted it from her hand, his mouth soft against her skin. He started chewing the apple, messily, bits falling on the ground. All the while looking at her. She breathed in, hardly able to believe she was standing here right next to him. She took another bite and held out the chunk to him. This time he didn't even sniff it, just took it from her greedily.

She reached out her hand to his neck and rubbed him slowly. He didn't move and, with her other hand, she gave him the rest of the apple. As he took it he jerked his head up quickly, his ears pricked forward.

'Hey!' She heard a voice behind her. 'Hey! That's my horse.'

She jumped backwards in fright, startling the horse, who stepped back sharply. She turned around. It was the boy from yesterday.

'Sorry, sorry, I only wanted to give him an apple I thought he was in trouble because he wasn't in the field and so I came down to find him in case he was hurt and then he wasn't and so I gave him an apple and I have two other apples he can have and I know he's your horse because I saw you on him but I also love him and my name's Ella and I'm sorry.' She drew breath.

The boy frowned at her. 'He's not hurt, he's fine and he's got lots of grass here and water, look.'

Ella was puzzled. 'I know that I just thought he'd like a treat and I shouldn't have come down here without asking you but I thought there was something wrong and then he was happy to see me so I stayed here and I was rubbing his neck and he didn't mind and –'

She stopped, as the boy was staring at her. Whenever she was thinking difficult thoughts she tumbled over her words and forgot to remind herself that there were such things as commas and full stops.

'I was hiding him in case you called the pound man.'

'The pound man? Like the dog pound?' Ella said, still puzzled.

'No. The horse pound. It's the place where they kill horses.'

'Kill them?' Ella said, her heart starting to thump, and her hand automatically reaching out to the horse as if to protect him. 'What d'you mean?'

He shrugged impatiently. 'I mean that. They take them away from us and then they kill them, that's what they do.'

Ella turned and looked at the horse. He had one ear forward and one backward. As if he was listening.

'And you think I'd call someone to come and kill him?'

she said, her voice shaking. 'I'd never do that. Never,' she said to the boy. 'I just want to come and see him. And I don't understand. Can't the guards stop them doing that if you tell the guards that people are stealing horses and killing them?'

'The guards help them sometimes, I can't call them. And how do I know it's true that you won't tell the pound?'

'Because …' Ella said, feeling sick to the pit of her stomach, 'because I never even knew there was such a thing and I love him. I love animals. I wish he was mine. You're lucky to have him. I would never ever hurt him.'

He looked down at his feet. 'How do I know that's true?'

Ella felt like shouting at him, but she didn't. 'You don't know,' she said, 'but I'm not a liar so you can believe me or not believe me, I don't care. But it's true anyway.'

For some reason that seemed to persuade him.

'You can see him so, but you can't ride him. His name is Storm because he was born in the rain and he's a keepsake of my grandma because she's dead now.'

'Oh, no,' Ella said, having heard enough about killing and death to last her a lifetime, and not quite knowing what to say next.

The boy just looked at her.

'Sorry,' she said quietly, trying to remember the proper words, 'Sorry for your losing her.'

He shrugged, not looking at her.

'Did she own the horse?' she asked.

'No. She was an old lady.'

'But then … what d'you mean a keepsake?'

'It's to remember her by. I got him when she died so that when I look at him I think of her. Like a photo but not on paper or anything. And if he goes to the pound, then –' he shrugged his shoulders – 'then it's like she's gone too.'

Ella scrunched her eyes up. She wished he would stop talking about the pound. When she opened them he was still standing there looking at her.

'So,' she said, handing him the bag of apples, 'every time you see him he'll remind you, even though if she was your granny you'll always remember her because you can't forget a granny, and I'm Ella,' she said, remembering too late that she'd already told him that. 'You give him the apples.'

'Johnny,' he mumbled as he unhooked the rope from the trees.

He took the bag and turned back towards Storm. 'Thanks.'

Ella lost her words when she wasn't either arguing her case or troubled, so she left and started walking back up the field to the gate.

All she could think of was that there was somewhere in Ireland where they killed horses. Horses like Storm. Like Molly and Giant. That thought filled her brain to almost bursting point. She wished it had never arrived there.

The Horse and his Boy

Johnny stood next to Storm and watched as Ella walked away and climbed over the gate. He shook his head. She could certainly talk. He hadn't expected to find her here. Storm ambled out from behind the trees and then picked up his pace as he realised he was now free. He set off at a fast gallop across the grass, kicking his legs up in the air as he went. When he reached the gate he reared up on his hind legs and let out a loud whinny. Ella turned and looked at him. Johnny couldn't be sure but it looked like she was clapping her hands. A funny girl, but he thought he believed her when she said she wasn't going to call the pound. She'd definitely not heard of it, she looked like she was going to cry when he told her about it. Maybe Storm was still safe.

He whistled. A special whistle he had just for Storm. Low and long. When Storm was just a foal he'd taught him to come with the whistle by holding a small scoop of feed and shaking it at the same time as he whistled. Now he didn't need the feed, and the horse came to him anyway.

That was the way it was with him and Storm. A pair of eejits, his mam called them. He watched as Storm trotted down the field towards him and stopped right in front of him. He reached into his pocket and pulled out a mint to give him. He then hooked the lead rope onto the halter and swung himself up onto his back.

When Storm was two, his da had suggested that he be trained as a sulky racer but Johnny had refused. It wasn't that he didn't like sulkies, he did, but he wanted Storm for himself. To ride and to be kept out in a field. He didn't want him in a stable where he couldn't run or scratch himself against the trees or buck or rear. He hated to think of him trapped in the darkness with nothing to do. He hated the dark himself and was glad of the street light outside on the road that shone in to where he slept. The older ones didn't mind but his two younger brothers were the same as him. The dark didn't suit them.

His da had agreed to let him decide what to do with Storm because of his grandma. Because he missed her even more than Johnny did. She was too young to die, he said, too young. And while Johnny didn't really understand then, as he was only eight when she died, he understood now. A good age to die would be much, much older than his grandma had been.

Tired Eyes

Ella chatted to the dogs (and to herself) the whole way back to the house. 'Who would kill horses? How do they kill them? Imagine that, Annie, killing horses. I suppose I eat dead animals, cows and lambs and pigs and someone killed them. I'm never eating them again. You hear me, Grouse? Never again. How could I eat a cow and then cry for a horse being killed? I'm telling Granny when I get back. Imagine if I ate you, any of you, that would be so cruel. And you have eyes and ears and paws and a tail and a brain and a heart and everything like me except for the paws and the tail. That's it, no more meat. And why did I rattle away talking to Johnny? He must think I'm mad. Before I go there again I'm going to practise talking normally. Hi Johnny. How are you? How is Storm today? Are you going to ride him again? Aren't you scared of getting on his back. I think I would be scared but maybe you can show me how and then I can learn as I've always wanted to learn but for some reason Granny doesn't want me to. She says she has her reasons but she won't tell me what they are even though

I have asked her a hundred times, even a thousand times perhaps? No. No. No. You're doing it again, Ella. Even practising you can't get it right. Johnny'll run a mile when he hears me and then I'll never get anywhere near Storm.'

She reached the back door and heard her granny talking to someone. As she came around the corner, she saw that Granny was on Skype talking to her dad. She ran in and stuck her head over her granny's shoulder.

'Hi, Dad, I'm back.'

He grinned. 'I can see that. Granny tells me you've been visiting a horse – you're not going anywhere near him?'

'Noooo … I'm always careful,' she said, as a memory came into her head of herself running down the field towards Storm. 'I'm not getting on his back or anything anyway. I'm not even good at riding so I wouldn't be able to unless someone here would teach me or take me to a riding place. You can ride horses dad why don't you come back and teach me?' Tears unbidden came into her eyes. She hated when she cried talking to her dad which was why mostly she preferred texting him. 'Sorry, Dad, I've just been running so I'm tired and my eyes just water when I'm tired.' She laughed. If anything fitted the description of a hollow laugh this one did, she thought. She had always wondered what one would sound like but now she knew, like a laugh that wasn't supposed to be there. He didn't answer her right away but her granny leaned towards the screen and patted where his head was – she always did that – and then she stood up. 'I'll be in the garden. You and Ella chat, and send some of that sunshine over here, will you, not too much, just a little so my lettuces can get a start in life'.

Ella's dad waved back and Ella sat down in the chair.

'Are you spending the whole summer with Granny this year or will you go back up to Mum for some of it?'

Ella thought for a moment. 'I think the whole summer? It's nicer here than Dublin, and Mum can come down if she wants but she can leave Damien behind.'

Her dad smiled. 'I'm sure he's not that bad, Ella,' he said.

'I wouldn't like someone to describe me as not that bad, Dad! He's not mean, he's just so boring, and Mum gets boring when he's around, she does nothing. At least here I'm with Granny and the dogs and everything. And Dad?'

He nodded. 'Yes, petal?'

'I was thinking you know that it might be a good idea for me to live here and when you come back you can live here also and get work somewhere near here and Mum can come and visit us? That might be a good idea.' She watched as her dad started to say something. 'Don't answer now, Dad. Granny says we have the whole summer to think about it so maybe you can as well? I haven't said it to Mum yet.'

'You'll miss Mum, won't you?'

'Well, I don't really miss her when I'm here for the whole summer and it's not like I won't see her. I'll see her more often than I see you anyway,' Ella said, regretting the words the minute she spoke them, but knowing she couldn't really take them back. If only she had a DELETE button.

'I know,' her dad said quietly. 'That won't be for long now, I promise. I'll talk to Granny about it.'

'And anyway lots of grannies look after their grandchildren and they're the best to do it because they've got a lot more experience than mums and dads because they've done it all before and so they know everything. Granny does and she told me yesterday she's not even that old so it'd be no bother to her at all she loves me and I help her because I take the dogs walking every day and if I wasn't here who could she tell her stories to?'

Her dad smiled. 'That's true. But I would still have to talk to her and Mum just to see what they think. OK?'

'OK.'

'So I'll say bye. I'm going to sleep. And I'll call you on the weekend. And be careful round that horse, you promise me, sweetie?'

'Yes, Dad. For the second time. I promise I'll be careful.'

She waved at him, then clicked END CALL. She always hated clicking that button because he just disappeared from sight and it felt wrong somehow. One minute it was as if he was in the room, the next minute he wasn't anywhere.

My Lovely Horse

'Granny?' Ella said.

'Yes, petal.'

'Why don't you have horses on the farm any more? I think you'd like to.' Without waiting for an answer, she carried on: 'And, Granny, how long do horses live?'

'There was a horse called Old Billy and he lived I think in the 1800s. He lived older than any known horse before or since; he was sixty-two when he died. But I think my favourite was an Irish Draught cross called Shayne. He was a rescue horse in England and he only died two years ago aged fifty-eight. Imagine that! Black Molly was twenty-eight when she died. That's not as young as it sounds. You can work it out in human years. A four-year-old horse is like a twenty-year-old human. More or less. Then for each year they live after that you add two and a half years. So work it out. Twenty plus twenty-four times two and a half?'

Ella grabbed a pen and scribbled on the newspaper. 'Wow. She was actually eighty years old.'

'Exactly. So not too young, not too old. Most horses,

if they're cared for, live until they're about thirty of our years. She didn't do too badly. And d'you know your dad knew her when he was very young. He probably doesn't remember but he did. She died when he was three.'

'And Giant, when did he die?'

'I can't remember right now how old he was, but don't worry about all that. I promised to tell you another story, and I'll do that while we eat our dinner.'

'But ...' Ella said, puzzled because she knew that that the age that Giant had died was definitely not something her granny would forget. Not in a million years.

'But nothing, petal. You want a story? Answer me quickly, as the offer is running out.'

She couldn't have made it more obvious that this was something she didn't want to talk about, so Ella just nodded and sat down on the wooden chair next to her. She looked surreptitiously at the thoughts above her granny's head, and thought she saw Giant standing there. Not moving.

'You ready?' her granny said.

Ella nodded and clicked RECORD on her phone. She stored her thoughts away for another time.

> When I was fifteen years old I was allowed to ride Black Molly by myself in the fields and on the roads. The roads were much quieter then so I'd sometimes go onto them but mostly I rode in the fields. The Meaneys and Roches, who were our neighbours back then and are still our neighbours now, let me go through their fields when there

weren't any cattle in them. One of the days I was riding along when I heard a strange noise in the ditch. A moaning noise. I got quite a fright because we always thought there was a ghost that walked around our townland. Usually it spent time in the twelve-acre field and I was far from that, but I knew ghosts could travel anywhere. It's not as if they'd get tired, they're dead already. Anyway, the noise was getting louder and Black Molly was starting to get a bit fidgety. I listened again and realised that it sounded a little like a cow.

So I jumped down off Molly and led her in the direction of the sound. In between the brambles and buttercups down in the ditch was a young cow mooing pitifully. It was stuck. I was in the Meaneys' field at that stage so I jumped back onto Molly's back and we galloped towards their house to tell them.

Old man Meaney was there and usually he would use his old Massey Ferguson 135 for things like this. But that day he couldn't as it was broken. I saw him looking at Black Molly. She was 16.3 hands high and very strong – she definitely had a mix in her of Clydesdale and Irish Draught. 'What d'you think Orla?' he said, 'd'you think your horse would be up for the job? The one down the ditch is only a heifer, she's not that big.'

You know what a heifer is, Ella?

'A young cow,' Ella said, a little insulted that her granny would even ask.

'Well, I thought about it. Black Molly was very strong and I knew horses were used to pull things before tractors took over, so I agreed.

We headed back towards the heifer, me back on Black Molly and old man Meaney walking along beside me carrying a rope and a battered blanket. I wasn't sure what that was for but didn't ask. He wasn't a talkative man. When we got there the poor heifer was bawling. Old man Meaney jumped down into the ditch beside her. She was still thrashing around, it was quite scary. She seemed to calm down after a while and let him put the strap around her belly. He then threw the rest of the strap up to me so that I could hold it while he pulled himself up.

Once he was up, old man Meaney started working the strap around Black Molly's chest, and where it was flat against her chest he used the torn blanket to pad it.

'Now,' he said, 'you're going to lead the horse slowly and I'm going to make sure the wee heifer is alright down in the ditch. Keep these straps stable as we don't have a proper harness. Keep her going very steadily, no fast movements.' I started leading her slowly forward and I could feel her leaning in once she realised that there was a weight pulling on her. Slowly we inched forward and I looked back when I heard old man Meaney shouting, 'Hey, hey, hup hup,' and I caught sight of the heifer's head appearing near the tip of the ditch. 'Come on Moll' I whispered, 'Come on girl, we're nearly there.' As I spoke I felt her jerk forward and I looked back in terror, but no need as the heifer was out and standing. I stroked Black Molly's head as old man Meaney started removing the straps, first from the heifer then from her.

He tipped his hat towards me. 'You're a topper,' he said, looking in his pockets for something to give me. He found his pipe and a half-crown. He gave me both. I gave him back the pipe but he wouldn't take the money back. 'And you,' he said, patting Black Molly's rump before he headed off out of the field, 'are a good girl.'

And she was, wasn't she good, petal?

Ella nodded.

'She was my best friend, you know,' Ella's granny said, patting Ella's arm. 'Some people think that's strange but it was true.'

Ella looked at her. 'I know, Granny. And I don't think it's strange.' She clicked the RECORD button off. 'I was thinking, you know, if I did come to live on the farm with you, maybe we could get two horses, one for you and one for me, so they have each other for company and you could teach me to ride. Maybe? Then you wouldn't miss Black Molly as much or Giant.'

'We still haven't decided about you coming to live here, petal, have we? If we decide, and it's a huge if, then we'll talk about that.'

Ella was never very good at stopping a train of thought once it had started.

'We don't even have to buy them. We could foster horses. There's this organisation in Dublin and they rescue horses. They're called My Lovely Horse Rescue, and they find horses that have been abandoned or thrown out into the forests or beaten and they rescue them and they're always looking for people to help. We could be a mini My Lovely Horse Rescue in Carrigcapall because you know all about looking after them and riding them and everything anyone would want to know, ever. We could even end up with more than two because we have all these fields and they're just lying empty all over the place.'

'Ella,' her granny interrupted, 'slow down. No decisions reached yet. We'll talk about this another day.'

'And you told me that Carrigcapall means Rock of the Horse, so it's a perfect place to have it in. You have to agree with that.'

'Ella, enough.'

Ella's granny wasn't a granny who shouted or even raised her voice, but when she spoke extra quietly Ella knew that it was time to stop.

Shoeing Tiny

Johnny sat in the yard with his da, who was trimming Penny's and Tiny's hooves. Penny was the biggest horse in the place, as her mother was a thoroughbred. She was fifteen hands, a piebald and the same age as Storm. Tiny was only as high as Penny's hocks, maybe a little higher and, since Magic had been taken, she was now the oldest horse they had. She was very bold. His dad had always told him that the smaller the horse, the bolder it got, and one look at Tiny and you'd know that was true.

Johnny loved watching his da trimming hooves and shoeing the horses. He loved the sound of the hammer against the anvil, and the way the horses stood so patiently. The dogs loved watching as well, but mainly because they were waiting for the treat of a bit of hoof that they could carry off and chew on for hours. His dog, Lucky, sat next to him, his mouth open.

'Da,' he said, 'there was a girl round Storm's field today.'

His da stopped hammering. 'What?'

Johnny shrugged. 'A girl was there. She said her name's Ella.'

'What did she want?'

'Dunno. She seems to just like looking at Storm. I told her about Magic and she knew nothing about the pound or anything.'

'So she says.'

'Yeah. But -'

'You watch that horse, boy. He's yours, you mind him. There's nothing I can do if he gets taken and they ask for nine hundred bucks to get him back. Nothing.'

'I know,' Johnny said. 'I do watch him. I hid him the other day behind the trees but then she came into the field.'

His da carried on with his work and shrugged his shoulders. 'Your business, boy. Just be careful is all I'm saying. Hand me that rasp yoke, then go and bring two of the others in from the field. I'm nearly done with this little gurrier.'

Tiny objected and gave a couple of kicks in his direction with her half-shod foot. He didn't shout at her. He just picked up the wriggling leg again and carried on. No horse, big or small, ever got the better of Johnny's da.

Johnny walked off down the road, doubts crowding into his head. What if Ella was lying? What if she had gone that minute and looked up the phone number and phoned them? Maybe the goons with the cattle trailer and no sense of how to handle horses were already coming to pick up Storm. He felt sick to his stomach and shouted for his little brother.

'Hey, Mikey, go and fetch the next two for Da. I have to go to Storm. Get the two handy ones from the layby, and then when I'm back I'll get the others. Now!'

Mikey threw his bike on the ground and headed off, delighted, because usually Johnny got all the best jobs.

Johnny set off at a run down the road, his heart bumping in his thin chest.

When he reached the gate, he stood up on the railing and looked down the field. At first he couldn't see his horse, but then he saw him grazing just to the left of the trees. He whistled, and Storm picked his head up and pricked his ears forward. Johnny jumped over the gate and started running towards him. He didn't know what he'd do if anyone ever took him.

An Empty Field

Ella resisted going to Storm's field for a few days. It was hard, but she felt somehow that she should leave him and the boy in peace. Before Johnny had arrived there she'd imagined that Storm was hers. She'd pictured him in the paddock in front of her granny's house, lifting his sweet head up when he saw her in the mornings, trotting towards her. She knew this was wrong but no-one else knew what was in her head, except perhaps her granny. Her granny was someone she definitely had to guard her thoughts from. Not that she'd be mad if she knew, because they were only thoughts, but even from her there were things she wanted to keep secret.

Last night her dad had texted her:

Sweetie-pie,
remember what I said
about the horse.
Mind yourself.

She had to think hard about a reply because her first thought was to say *Stop telling me that*, but she'd learned to not always go with her first thought. To keep it trapped in her head for just a little while before it escaped wildly from her mouth. It didn't always work. But it was easier with texts because he couldn't watch her as she struggled with the words. Her reply was

I will, Dad.

On the fourth day she couldn't resist the pull of it any longer, and she set off to go and see him. Maybe Johnny would be there and he wouldn't mind. When she reached the gate, she saw that it was hanging open, almost as if it had been pulled from its hinges. The field was empty. She ran down in the direction of the clump of trees where she'd found him previously. Nothing. He'd gone. She started jogging towards the furthest corner of the field; maybe he'd escaped. Stallions were hard to keep in a field, her granny had always told her. If there were mares in season they'd want to get to them. She peered through the dense gorse bushes to the field beyond but he wasn't there. She stood still catching her breath; maybe Johnny had taken him somewhere else because he didn't trust her.

Suddenly she heard a yell and she turned to see Johnny running towards her waving his arms and shouting. He had a rope in one hand and a bucket in the other. Annie started barking at him as he came closer but he ignored her. He came to a stop right in front of Ella.

'What did you do to him?' he shouted. 'Where's he gone? Where's Storm?'

Ella took a step backwards. 'Nothing. I didn't do anything, I only just got here, what's wrong, where's he gone? I thought you took him, it wasn't me, how could it be me?' She stared at Johnny and to her surprise she saw tears rolling down his cheeks.

'He was here,' he said. 'Last night he was right here. I gave him a feed and filled up the water and now the gate's open, it's broken. And look,' he said, pointing at the ground. Ella looked down and saw tyre tracks pressed into the earth.

'What's happened?' she said, not wanting to hear the answer.

'What d'you think? My da warned me. He told me; I didn't listen.'

'Told you what?'

'That I should be careful. I don't know who you are. Did you call the pound man? Or the guards?'

Ella shook her head furiously. 'No, I told you I'd never even heard of him or them or whoever they are. And why the guards? I did nothing, I just came to see him.'

He shook his head. 'But he's gone,' he said, spreading his hands, 'gone. And the gate, pulled off, it's them I tell you. It's the pound man, I know.' Fresh tears started from his eyes and he rubbed them away angrily.

Ella felt sick to her stomach. 'What can we do?' she said. 'Maybe someone saw them taking him? Or maybe he just jumped over the gate and broke it or something.'

Johnny shook his head. 'Don't be stupid – he's been here for ever.' Before Ella could answer, he carried on. 'And anyways they'd take him in the night so no-one would see them, not even Delaney.' He looked at her, frowning. 'Did you tell anyone else about him?'

Ella hesitated. 'My granny, but she only knows I come here to see him, and,' she said, suspecting the direction his thoughts were headed in, 'she would never say anything to anyone. And – I'm not stupid.'

He threw his hands up in the air. 'OK OK – but you shouldn't have told her. I'm going to tell my da,' he said as he started walking away. 'You know something, we only have five days till they kill him. That's all.'

'Wait! Five days? Why? What's the point of that?'

He turned. 'I don't know. It's just what they do.'

'I'll help you, Johnny. I promise I did nothing. I want to help get him back, I'll do anything.'

He stared at her as if making his mind up.

He shook his head. 'Well, come back here after dinner. Don't bring anyone else. Not even your granny.'

She nodded. 'OK.'

With that he left, the rope slung over his shoulder and the bucket hanging by his side. Ella watched as he walked away, his back hunched. Tears started in her own eyes as she thought of Storm being taken away to the place where they killed horses.

Hard Things in this World

Johnny looked back at her when he reached the gate. She hadn't moved; she was just standing there patting the whippet. He didn't want to go home; he didn't want to tell his da because he'd warned him. It was hard to believe her but why would she have come back to the empty field if she'd called the pound? And he'd seen the way she looked at Storm the first time he met her. He'd seen her face when he told her about the pound and the way they kill the horses. He wished he hadn't cried in front of her though, but he couldn't help it. If Storm was gone then there was nothing left of his grandma. It was as if she'd been taken all over again. If Storm had gone, where would he go every day after school?

He carried on walking towards home, his head heavy. If Storm had been taken by the pound, then all he had was five days. Five days to save him. He remembered the day they came to take some of the others from the herd. Blackie and Sally, two miniatures, both heavy in foal. He remembered the men chasing them around the field on their quad bikes till they were too tired to escape. Then the shouting and herding them into the cattle trailer, their eyes wide with fear. He heard later that Blackie had foaled in the trailer. The foal born dead. And five days later Blackie was too. And Sally. He remembered his dad telling him and Mikey how the pound killed the horses, a bolt gun to the head. He couldn't let them do that to Storm. He closed his eyes and imagined Storm in the same trailer all the way down to Kiltermon where the pound was. Trapped inside the metal box, swaying from side to side because they didn't care.

When he finally reached home his da was sitting outside the house sorting out the bucket of horseshoes and pulling old nails out of them. He didn't look up as Johnny came towards him. Johnny didn't think any more about what he had to say, nothing could make it come out better.

'They've taken Storm – the pound man came and took him.'

His da looked up. 'You saw them?'

'No. I saw nothing, but he's gone, the gate's hanging open and there's tyre tracks.'

'It's that girl. I told you, Johnny, you shouldn't have talked to her.' He threw the hammer on the ground. 'Again. How many horses do they want from us?'

'No, it's not the girl. I saw her there; she was looking for him too.'

His da stared at him. 'I can't get him back, Johnny. Nine hundred plus they'll be asking for him. I haven't that kind of money.'

'But Delaney said you could use that field. You told me that they can't take him if we've permission?'

'They can do anything they bloody like. They took Magic; she was in the same place.'

'But if Delaney tells them we have the permission?'

'They'll just say he was out on the road. He's gone, Johnny; you may get used to it.'

'But what about Grandma? If we tell them he's a keepsake of Grandma, maybe they'll bring him back then?'

His da laughed, a harsh laugh. He stared out towards the road. 'You think they care about that? There's things, hard things in this world. I've delayed too long in telling you about them, boy.' He went back to the horseshoe in his hand.

Johnny stood there for a few more minutes, then turned and left, his heart like a small heavy stone inside his chest.

He started walking back to the field. Maybe he was wrong. Maybe someone had left the gate open and Storm had wandered out looking for grass. He might be back. There was a chance. He walked slowly; he was in no rush to get there, knowing in his heart that no matter how hard he wished, Storm wouldn't be there. His grandma used to tell him that there was no point starting something if you weren't going to finish it, because a world full of unfinished things was a useless world. If she was here still she'd help him try to get Storm back. She'd start looking for him and then she would finish. The problem was he didn't know where to start. Maybe the girl would come back this afternoon – she'd said she would. He'd wait there in the field till the afternoon, and maybe the two of them could come up with something.

Four Hundred and Thirty-two Thousand Seconds

'Granny, Granny!' Ella shouted as she opened the back door and ran into the kitchen. 'Where are you?'

The door to the back pantry flew open.

'What's happened, petal? You all right?' her granny said, her face startled and worried.

'I'm all right, Granny,' Ella said, breathless from running most of the way back, 'but Storm's not all right, you know the horse in the field with the boy who jumped on his back the one that might be related to Black Molly, the horse not the boy, well he's gone. Completely gone. And the boy, his name is Johnny, he thinks the pound man came and took him and that means they'll kill him. There were tyre tracks and the gate was hanging open nearly off its hinges we didn't know why it was open it was as if someone just bashed it in to steal him and ...' Ella stopped and shook her head. 'And Johnny was there and first he thought I called the pound man and he called me stupid but I don't mind because he was upset and crying, but I told him I didn't and I think he believes me and he was mad I had told you so I shouldn't even be telling you now but I don't know what to do.'

Her granny closed the door behind her, but not before Ella had caught a glimpse of what looked like the corner of a bed in the pantry.

'Granny?'

'Yes, petal.'

'That room –'

'Don't be worrying your head about that room, petal,' her granny interrupted her. 'Slow down. The horse is definitely gone?'

'Yes. Johnny looked everywhere. I said I'd go back after dinner to see him, to see what we can do.'

'Take a breath, petal,' her granny said, sitting down at the table. 'I'm not sure you should be getting involved in this.'

'Granny! They're going to kill him and they shouldn't have took him –'

'Taken,' her granny said.

'Whatever, they shouldn't have done it because he doesn't belong to them and Johnny needs help. We have to help him.'

'Slow down. You won't be able to do anything if you just rush around like a mad thing. Stop a bit and think.'

Ella sat down and watched as her granny put the kettle onto the Aga. 'We don't have a lot of time, Granny,' she said. 'Five days, if no-one gets Storm from the pound then he'll be killed. And there's nothing wrong with him. He's not hungry, Johnny looks after him, he's a happy horse or he was a happy horse …'

Her granny patted her on the head. 'Five days is longer than you think, petal. It's a hundred and twenty hours. And then if you multiply that by sixty – try it, there's my calculator – you would get?'

Ella breathed in. She didn't feel like doing calculations but she knew her granny and if she didn't they wouldn't move to the next step, which hopefully would be her granny agreeing to help. If she didn't agree then Ella would do whatever had to be done by herself; nothing was going to stop her. She reached for the calculator and punched the numbers in. 'Seven thousand two hundred minutes, and that means …' she said, pressing the buttons for times sixty again, as she knew that'd be the next request, 'four hundred and thirty-two thousand seconds, which is fine, Granny, but at least six hundred of those seconds have passed while I've been sitting here doing this.'

Her granny smiled. 'OK, petal, let's see what we can do.'

Ella grinned. 'Yes! I knew you'd help us.'

'I'm not promising anything, but let's work out where we are. Grab a pen and paper and let's work out what we have to do. So, Storm was in the field, the one that belongs to Delaney?'

Ella nodded.

'Write that down as number one.'

Ella did what she was asked, knowing from the set of her granny's shoulders, that resistance was futile.

'What is Johnny's other name, his surname?'

Ella shrugged. 'I didn't ask him.'

'Well, that's number two: Find out Johnny's surname so we can track down his parents. Now, number three, describe the horse to me.'

'He's black, you know that, he's as tall as about three-quarters of the door in height, quite tall. He has a long mane and tail, and they're also black.'

'About 14.2 hands, then. You know why they measure horses in hands, Ella?'

'No,' Ella said, not wanting to know right now but realising she was about to be told. Sometimes her granny wore her out with information.

'It started in ancient Egypt when a hand was used to measure things, mainly I suppose because they didn't have measuring tapes. So one hand was equal to either four fingers flat out or a clenched fist – or ten centimetres, but for horses that doesn't sound as nice. So we use hands. And lastly, number four, is he a stallion or a gelding or even a mare?'

Ella frowned, not sure why any of this mattered at all when Storm was trapped somewhere waiting to die.

'Johnny talks about him as a he, so he's one of those two things, but just not a mare. A gelding is when he can't, you know, be a dad?'

Her granny laughed. 'That's about it, Ella; they have an operation. And, you see, if he's a stallion he's always on the lookout for mares. Which is why a stallion is often kept by himself.'

'Well, then, I think he's that,' Ella said.

'Double-check that for me, will you?' her granny said. 'And one last one, number five. Ask Johnny does the horse have a chip? When you get a passport for a horse, the vet puts a microchip in its neck and you can scan the chip if a horse is lost to see who owns it. If he has a chip that's great – it makes everything easier.'

Ella wrote that down. 'It must hurt when they do that, put the chip in?'

'It does but it's just like an injection which hurts for a little bit then goes away.'

'What's number six, Granny? We need a number six so we know what to do? All the other things are just asking questions, not doing anything.'

'Number six is to make yourself a sandwich because you can't do anything if you haven't food in you, and when you come back with answers we can go onto number seven.'

As Ella did what she'd been told to do, she thought about the list. It was better than nothing, but whatever her granny said it was still just a long list of questions. No matter what the answers were they wouldn't save Storm. And when she went back to Johnny she'd have to explain why she was asking him so many questions; then she'd have to explain about her granny. That wouldn't be easy.

So Many Questions

When Ella arrived Johnny was already there, mooching around the field, kicking at the ground. He looked up when he heard Grouse barking. When she reached him he looked at her and tilted his head to one side.

'Well,' he said, 'you came back.'

She frowned. 'I said I would.'

He shrugged. 'Not everyone always does what they say. My dad says there's nothing he can do. The pound wants too much money. And they won't listen, we've tried before.'

'Well –'

'Well what?'

'I know I said I wouldn't speak to my granny but I did because I don't know what else to do right now so she asked me some questions and I'm going to ask you them.'

'What's the point of questions?'

'I don't know but maybe there's something that'll help. She knows the farmer from this field.'

'Delaney?'

Ella nodded, deciding to push ahead with the questions before Johnny decided not to answer.

'This is Delaney's field, right?'

'Yeah, and he gave my da permission to keep the horse here.'

Ella ticked that off the list.

'And what's your surname?'

'My surname? What's that got to do with anything?'

'I don't know. But you own him, so?'

'I do, but he's in my da's name.'

'What's your dad's surname?'

'Joyce. Same as mine. What's yours?'

'Mackey is my dad's surname but my mum is Quinn. She lives in Dublin and my dad is in Australia but he's coming back soon.' Ella shook her head. It all sounded too complicated and she didn't want to think about any of it right now. She looked back down at her list. 'So, is Storm a stallion or a gelding or a mare?'

'A stallion. He covered three mares this year. I'll get one of the foals off my uncle's mare.'

'And how tall is he?'

'14.2. This is stupid, it won't get him back.'

'I don't know,' Ella said, 'but Granny asked for it and she said she'll help us.'

'Isn't she too old to help?'

'No. She's medium old, but she's clever and she knows a lot about horses; she used to have horses long ago. She's not a horrible person.'

'There's nothing she can help us with. Da said they won't

give him back unless we pay. And anyway the pound is in Kiltermon.'

'What?' Ella said. 'Why's it all the way down there?'

'It just is.'

Ella looked at Johnny, hating how she could still see smudged tears on his face.

'That's terrible. Because even if we decided to go and look for him we can't.'

He nodded.

Ella looked down at her list, feeling hopeless. 'Also, I forgot, is he chipped?'

Johnny nodded. 'Chipped and licensed, but that doesn't matter, they took horses before that were chipped. Even ones we showed them the books of.'

'The books?'

'Passports, horse passports. That's their books.'

'Granny says if he has a chip then we can be sure that it's him.'

'I'd know it was him anyway. You could put a thousand horses in a field, I'd know him. But I'll get his book and then we can see. D'you have money saved?'

'About twenty-seven euro, maybe.'

'I have eleven. We can get a bus ticket to Kiltermon and find him. I've been there before. To the pound.'

'Maybe,' Ella said doubtfully, 'but then if he is we can't bring him back on the bus.'

'I know, I'm not stupid, we can just phone my da to fetch him.'

'OK, but ...'

He looked at her. 'Maybe we can get a lawyer even. I think my da knows one. I have to go home to help Da with the other horses, we're moving them so they don't get taken as well. I'll bring the papers tomorrow and my money. From tomorrow it's only four days left,' Johnny said, turning to leave.

As Ella walked home she started trying to picture what the pound looked like. She'd been once to the dog pound and seen the dogs in cages, but you couldn't keep horses that way. She hoped that none of the horses could see the other horses being killed. Or even hear them. She shivered as she pictured a row of horses, Storm among them, watching over their stable doors as a little pony was being killed, each one of them knowing that they might be next.

She called the dogs close to her side, and for once they obeyed. She crouched down on the ground and put her arms around their necks. She'd asked Johnny whether the horse pound was like the dog pound without even thinking about what that meant. If they killed horses at the horse pound they must kill dogs at the dog pound. She looked at Annie and Grouse, tails wagging, looking at her as if to work out what was wrong. They knew something was wrong – they wouldn't usually stay still for so long. She could see the questions in their eyes.

She stood up, wanting to blank out all the awful thoughts in her head, and she started running home. She had all the information now, she thought, clutching the piece of paper tightly in her hand. Now all they needed to do was to work out a plan.

Keepsake

When Ella arrived home she found her granny sitting in the kitchen. She glanced at the door into what she now called the secret room, and saw that the key was in the lock. That had never happened before. She looked at her granny who just smiled. Ella decided not to ask her about it.

'I have the list, Granny. Yes, he has permission from Mr Delaney to keep the horse there, Storm is about 14.2 hands he has a chip he's a stallion and Johnny's surname is Joyce and he asked me if you're old and I said medium old but very clever and that you know a lot about horses and you're not horrible but it's not that he said you were I just wanted him to know you're not.'

'Ella,' her granny said, laughing, 'when you write in school, do you write the same way you speak?'

'Like how?'

Like one long stream of words one after the other.'

Ella shook her head. 'No. My teacher wants us to write proper sentences so my stories always come back full of red marks and she never says anything at all about what's in the story just about what's wrong I think the teachers here would be better Granny you know if I came down to live here and go to the school dad was in when he was my age?'

Without warning Ella saw a pool of sadness above her granny's head and watched her as she wiped her forehead, almost as if she was wiping the thoughts away.

'We'll talk about that, I promise, but we have a job to do now don't we? We need a new piece of paper,' she said, looking at the scrunched up piece lying on the table. 'Here,' she said, tearing off a piece from her notebook, 'Where were we, number five?'

'Yes, but number six was a sandwich,' Ella said, anxiously wishing the sadness would go away, which it did as her granny laughed.

'Number seven is to call Delaney to tell him. You're sure that the day before this happened the gate into the field was closed tightly?'

'I'm sure.'

'Right. If Delaney says that Johnny's dad, Joyce you said his name was, had permission, then –' She paused. 'I wonder if that's Annie Joyce's family. Did he say anything about his granny?'

'Yes. He calls her his grandma not granny and Storm is a keepsake of her.'

'A keepsake?'

'Yes, he said that when his grandma died then he got Storm as a keepsake of her so a little bit of her is in Storm so that he never forgets her. Her memory is in him.'

Her granny sat quietly and Ella saw, for the first time

ever, tears forming in her eyes. Her granny didn't even try to hide them.

'Sorry, petal, don't mind me, but that's beautiful. I'm not crying for sadness,' which Ella knew was true as she could see that the pool had not returned. 'It's just that's a good way to hold onto memories. I wonder if Annie was his grandma. I knew her you know, she used to come around here selling stuff, some of my pots, like the one we use for potatoes, came from her. In fact, there's a story about that pot I must tell you. I didn't think she was that old though, more like my age – medium old,' she said, smiling through her tears.

'I'll ask him, Granny, but we need to get back to the list.'

'Yes. Number seven. I can call Delaney and ask him about his field. It's quite far from his actual farm, on an out farm, so he might not have seen that the gate is hanging off. Number eight: we have to get a number for the council so we can find out who's in charge of the pound. You find that number and I'll phone them.' She looked at the clock on the far wall. 'It's too late now but if you find the number I'll phone them first thing tomorrow. I think that's enough of a plan for the moment. Then if you see Johnny in the morning you can tell him two things we've done.'

'I suppose,' Ella said, looking doubtful. 'But I don't think he wants to hear about more talking or lists of things. He wants – I want – to *do* something. You know, something that sets us on our way to save Storm?'

'I know, petal, but if we hear from Delaney and he says that he had permission to use the field then I can tell the council that, because it's the council who pay the pound to do this work, and they'll be the ones who give us permission to get Storm back. So that's not just words. That's something.'

'OK,' Ella said, unconvinced.

'So, if you lay the table for us and start boiling the eggs, I'll ring Delaney and you can listen while you work.' She picked up the phone and started dialling as Ella tried her hardest to lay the table without making a sound.

'Jimmy, Orla here.'

'Yes, all good. I have Ella with me.'

'No, he's not back yet, still over there, hopefully soon.'

'Jimmy, I just wanted to run something by you. You know the field you have near the road?'

'Well, have you it let to anyone?'

'Ah, that's good, was just checking. The little lad knows my Ella and the horse has been taken from the field, we think by the pound, so I just wanted to make sure.'

'Yes, yesterday, and Ella says the gate is hanging off as if it was forced off its hinges – you might want to check it.'

'I know, I know. I'll come back to you on it, we might need your help.'

She looked at the phone and frowned. 'Yes, Jimmy, I'm absolutely sure.'

Her granny waved as she put the phone back down. She always did that when she ended a conversation.

'OK, petal, that's a good start. He has the field let to Johnny's dad, so the pound had no business going in there and taking the horse. It must just be a mistake – maybe they thought he didn't have permission. I'll ring the council first thing in the morning and it'll all be sorted.'

'What are you absolutely sure about?' Ella asked.

'Nothing that matters. Jimmy is just like that; you have to tell him a story twice before he believes you. It can get a bit tiresome to be honest.'

The Burnt Potato Pot

After they'd cleared away the tea and fed the dogs, Ella's granny suggested they sit in the garden and she'd tell her a story. The evening was bright and warm. Just outside the back door, near the hawthorn tree, there was a wooden bench and an upturned granite trough. Ella used that for a seat while her granny sat on the bench. Annie and Grouse leapt up onto the trough next to Ella and settled down, for all the world as if they were getting ready to listen. Old Greg wasn't around. Ella looked up into the branches and a solitary magpie was sitting there looking down at her. It tilted its head to one side, and she felt a slight shiver run down her back and looked away.

'Granny,' Ella said before her granny had a chance to say anything, 'can you make it a happy story? I don't want to hear about anyone dying, horses or dogs or cats or humans, not even beetles or flies.'

'Happy it is,' her granny said.

'Oh, and I forgot to tell you. I've decided I'm not going to eat meat any more, ever again in my life. Never. I've dccided I don't want animals killed just so I can have a bacon sandwich or something like that. Imagine if Grouse was killed and fried up? That would be awful.'

Her granny looked at her. 'You're becoming a vegetarian? Today?'

'Yes. No more meat or fish or chicken or anything. Do eggs count?'

'No, you can eat eggs, petal. But let's talk about that another day because we're not going to talk about anything dying, remember? Especially not poor old Grouse being fried up!'

Ella laughed. 'OK, but I mean it.'

'I don't doubt it for one minute, petal; stubbornness runs in the family. But here goes. I think I'm going to tell you a story about when your dad was a little boy.'

'I love those ones,' Ella said. 'They're my favourites. Them and Black Molly and Giant.'

'Right, so all you have to do is listen. And Mrs Joyce's potato pot comes into it, so it makes a little journey right back to where we are now. That's strange isn't it? Almost as if she was reminding me.'

'Maybe that's a good omen,' Ella said, and clicked on her RECORD button

Her granny smiled and started.

Your dad may not have told you this but when he was small he was very bold. He was like a mouse: you know how mice are quiet and can get into anything? You know about their collapsible skeletons?'

Ella nodded.

Well, he didn't have one of those, thank goodness, but for a long time I suspected he did. He just went everywhere. It was hard to keep him inside. Maybe mouse is the wrong word – are mice good climbers?'

'Not really, Granny, especially not on smooth surfaces; their little feet slip. But they can jump, even the house mice can jump and field mice.'

OK, so maybe he was like a field mouse, because it was hard to keep him inside. Anyway, by the time he was three years old he had so much energy that it was all I could do to keep up with him, so I put up a small fence around the back section of the garden and told him he couldn't go past it. It gave him plenty of room, if you look along there.

Her granny pointed to the beds.

The fence went to the end of the lawn and all the way round to the back door so he could run in and out whenever he felt like it. Except in winter because I had to keep the door shut because of the cold, then he had to ask me to open it. But the weather didn't seem to matter to him as long as he was out in it. Your grandfather said I should have put up an electric fence and that might have worked but I think, I hope, he was joking.

For the first year the fence worked very well. He played about happily with the dogs, we had Leo and Ginny back then, and during the summer I only saw him when he got hungry. So I got used to that and I suppose I stopped paying attention. It's never a good idea Ella to stop paying attention to anything. Ever.

Her granny sat up straighter and leaned over to stroke Ella's head.

Sorry, petal, this is a very long introduction. So, one day in June when the sun was shining and a small breeze was lifting the grass clippings, your dad headed out to play. He'd just turned five. He asked me if he could take some biscuits outside with him and I agreed, on condition that he didn't give any to the dogs, because if there is one thing I cannot abide it is a fat dog. I didn't think much of him asking me that because he was a boy who needed to eat.

Time passed and I busied myself with things, the usual kind of things. I baked the bread, did the washing, cleaned the kitchen and at some point I put on the dinner. At about half past twelve I looked out of the window and realised that he wasn't there. I remember thinking that perhaps he was tired and had come inside, so I went to check in his bedroom. He wasn't there. Perhaps, I thought, he was in the bushes around the back which were still inside the fenced area, so I went out the back to look. Nothing. No sign of him. And no sign of the dogs either. I called and whistled as by this time a small bit of panic had started to creep into my heart because of the silence. Not a bark, not a shout, not a whisper.

The fence was a wooden one and quite strong and not an easy one to climb over and the gate was on a latch that I had tied together with twine. When I came closer to it I saw that it had been carefully untied; in fact the twine was no longer even there. I ran down the back lane towards the humpy bumpy field, mainly because I hoped that he had wandered off in that direction rather than in the direction of the road. All I saw in the humpy bumpy field were Molly and Giant. Black Molly was very old by then and Giant only five years younger than her. They were standing in the shade of the tall ash tree. All this time I was whistling and calling. I had more hope of the dogs hearing me than your dad – he was prone from a young age to selective deafness. He heard what he wanted to hear, when he wanted to hear it. But nothing. No sound. I have never before nor since felt such a deep silence on the farm. Even

Black Molly and Giant didn't whinny when I came near them. It was as if a huge blanket of no noise had been thrown over the fields.

And I know I promised no sadness but by this time the tears were streaming down my face, every worst thought I could ever have was in my mind.'

Ella had no trouble believing that. The cloudy image of a little boy above her granny's head was very dark as she relived it all. At least she was sure it had a happy ending, as her dad was still around. Knowing that was like reading the last chapter of a book if you were worried about something happening to your favourite character.

I went into the triangle field. Same thing, nothing. Through into the rath field, nothing stirring other than the dandelions and the thistles. I don't know why I kept running in that direction, it was as if a madness had taken over my head. I stopped on top of where the rath used to be before someone not right in the head had bulldozed it down. You never do that, you know that, Ella. Never destroy a rath.

Ella nodded. This was something her granny had told her almost before she could walk.

I turned around and started walking back towards

the road, my heart and legs heavy. I couldn't run any more, my head felt like it was about to explode. I walked out of the gate and looked left and then right, trying to put myself into his bold little mind. Right was towards the main road and the shops, left was towards the Meaneys and chocolate. Old Mr Meaney had a sweet tooth you see and any time we visited he opened the third drawer in the kitchen and inside it was chocolate. Mr Meaney would let him choose a bar and then he'd open it and they'd share it. Your dad always used to ask me why I didn't have a third drawer. And why Mr Meaney's name didn't match who he was. Thinking about his deep interest in Mr Meaney I took a decision and went left.

I crossed the road and went into their yard. Everything was quiet. It was dinner time so perhaps they were all inside. I knocked on the back door, holding my breath, praying that he'd be inside. 'The door's open,' I heard a voice say. 'We're in the kitchen.' I pushed it open and went through and there they were, happy as Larry (although I've never learnt who Larry actually was and why he was always happy). Your dad and the dogs and Mr and Mrs Meaney, sitting around the kitchen table.

'Orla,' Mrs Meaney said, 'Mr Pat Mackey here –' and she patted your dad on the head – 'was telling us that now that he's five you let him come over to visit us on his own so long as he has the dogs with him, on a lead. And he's even allowed to cross the road on his own.'

I just stood there, not knowing what to say or do, and your dad sat there looking down at the table not knowing what to say or do either. The dogs ran towards me and I noticed they were tied together, the blue baling twine from the gate carefully knotted onto their collars. 'Well,' I said, finding my voice from somewhere deep inside my tummy, 'not exactly, Mrs Meaney, in fact, not in any which way that anyone in the whole world could think of. Mr Pat Mackey here is not allowed beyond the gate in the garden, the gate tied closed with this.' I pointed down to the blue twine.

Your dad looked up at me and I was, in truth, so relieved to see him, that I couldn't do anything other than call him to me and take him by the hand. 'We'll go home now and then Mr Pat Mackey and I will talk about all of that. Say thank you for your dinner, and ...' I said, seeing the chocolate wrapper lying abandoned on the table, 'the chocolate.' A very quiet voice mumbled 'thank you' and off we went. Me, your dad and the tied together dogs, back home to the kitchen. I had, in my panic, left the potatoes cooking, and by now the pot had burnt so badly that there are still little moon craters in the bottom of it. If you ever ask your dad about why that potato pot looks like that he'll definitely remember. So. A happy ending?'

'Yes, Granny,' Ella said, switching off the recording, 'a relieved ending. Imagine if something else had happened, I wouldn't be here today and then you'd have no-one at all.'

Her granny nodded. 'I know, petal – imagine that!'

Three Spoons of Sugar

Johnny woke up the following morning as soon as the sun showed itself. Four days left, that was all he had to save Storm. He went into the room where his mam and dad were sleeping.

'Da?' he called. 'Da, it's morning and we only have four days left.'

His da turned over and opened one eye. 'Johnny, four days, twenty days, it makes no difference.'

'But he's mine. They can't just take him. He's not their horse.'

'I know, son.' His da lay flat on his back looking at the ceiling, his lips pursed tight. Still not ready to tell Johnny the hard things about this world. 'But that's what they're doing these days. Better men than me have burst themselves trying to get their animals back.'

'Uncle Davey says you should go down with a few lads and break the horse out,' said Johnny then.

His da sat up. 'What did I tell you about your uncle Davey?'

'He has his own ways,' said Johnny, sorry now, 'and you have yours.'

'That's right, and his ways only make you feel like a man for a short while. His ways have no road back.'

Davey wasn't the only one who said that Johnny's da was too soft. Uncle Davey said he'd swing for any pound man that took his son's horse. But Johnny also knew that his uncle had no better idea of how to get a horse back from the pound than anyone did. He only had ideas about how to not lie down. Johnny wasn't going to say that now.

'It's best to try and put it out of your head. Things you can't change can drive you mad thinking about them.' His da turned over trying to put it out of his own head.

Johnny went out. He punched his fist into his palm in frustration. If his da couldn't do anything then no-one could, especially not an old lady he'd hardly met and Ella whom he hardly knew. He pulled on his track pants and walked outside. He pictured Ella counting off her list and writing down his answers. He didn't see how any of that could help Storm, except maybe if Delaney said something.

He walked back into his da's room.

'Can you phone Delaney when you get up because if he tells the pound man that you're allowed to keep your horses there then they have to give him back.'

'Yes, I'll phone him.' A muffled voice came out from under the blankets. 'But I'm not waking him up at five in the morning to ask him. Go back and see if you can get a bit of sleep, son.'

Johnny's heart lifted slightly. It was a better answer

than any of the others. It was a something rather than a nothing. He went back into the room he shared with his three brothers and stood up on his bed to reach the photo of Storm that his mam had taken to get framed. It was blurry but you could see him, he was barely a yearling, his legs long on his body. He was looking at the camera as if he knew someone was taking a photo.

Johnny took the picture and placed it carefully on top of the kitchen counter just in case his da forgot to phone Delaney. He pulled the sugar bowl next to it. His da put three spoons of sugar in his tea every morning so he would definitely see the picture.

'Johnny,' his da shouted from the other room, 'if you're not going back to sleep, feed the dogs, will you, and take Abby into the paddock.'

Johnny stepped outside without answering. Abby was his da's favourite mare. She was a brown and white four year old he'd bought up north. She was in foal to Storm. Johnny opened the stable door and called her. She walked towards him and bent her head down to sniff at his outstretched palm.

'Good girl, Abby,' he said, clipping the lead rope to her halter and rubbing her neck, 'come on.'

As he was leading her he thought of the foal inside her and wondered would it be black like its father or coloured like her. His uncle had one coloured stallion and he always threw coloured foals but Storm seemed to throw a mix of colours. Abby had had one coloured filly and a chestnut colt so far, so this one could be anything. It was funny the way things worked, a small memory of his grandma inside Storm and now an even smaller memory of her growing inside Abby. How big would it get to grow before someone took it away and killed it?

When he'd finished doling out the nuts and last night's crusts to the dogs, he sat for a while watching them. Shadow was his favourite after Lucky. He was the one that would go hunting with him in the summer. Shadow could walk all day and night and never get tired. He was a lurcher and black all over like Storm except for one patch of white over his eye. It was hard to think of anything that didn't come back to Storm. Johnny stood up. He'd get some breakfast and then head over to the field. Maybe Ella would be up early and they could make a plan.

He went back inside, grabbed two slices of bread and buttered them, then made sure the photo of Storm was still on the table and left. All of his brothers were still sleeping. The only sound in the house was the door banging shut behind him.

Pancakes and Cinnamon

That morning Ella was also up early. For once before her granny. This was the first time she could remember this happening. She'd looked up the council numbers the night before and had written them out carefully on a notepad that her granny kept next to the phone.

Finally, at half past seven, her granny came downstairs. 'You're up early, petal,' she said, 'did you get any sleep?'

'Of course I did,' Ella said, seeing as how she was one of those children who could put their head down on the pillow and fall into a deep and uncomplicated sleep. 'Did you?'

Her granny nodded. 'Yes. Except Old Greg was barking away at his magpies for half the night; it's no wonder he eats more than the other two put together – he never stops.'

'Have you ever thought –' Ella started saying, then shook her head thinking better of it. 'Never mind, here are the numbers for the council, Granny, lots of numbers. Not sure which number is for horses. Could it be Leisure or maybe Roads?' She handed her granny the list and the phone.

'They won't be in till nine at the earliest, petal,' her granny said, putting the phone back, 'we can call them then. We'll eat something; then you can take the dogs for a walk and then we'll phone them.'

Two hours away seemed like a lifetime to Ella. 'And you're sure they won't do anything to Storm in the meantime, Granny?'

'What did your friend Johnny say? He said that we have five days.'

Ella nodded, not sure if Johnny would be that pleased at being called her friend.

'Well, that's plenty of time. We're on day two and already we know about Delaney and we have the number for the council.'

Ella wished she could believe her granny. She shook her head. Breakfast. Dog walk. Keeping busy. That was the answer. If she was busy it stopped her thinking about the things she didn't want to think about. Maybe later she'd even chance asking her granny for another story if the time went too slowly.

'Maybe as we've got so much time we could have pancakes for breakfast? If I walk the dogs and you make the pancakes, because you make them faster than me ... then that will take up time.'

'It surely will.'

'And can I have the first pancake, the one that always goes wrong? Dad told me you used to always give him that one.' Ella turned to face her granny. 'Do you think he'll come back soon, Granny? He's not going to stay there for ever?'

'Of course he's not, petal. I know it's been a long time, too long, but I think he'll be back soon.'

Ella stared at her. 'Maybe he'll even be here by the end of summer?'

'Maybe. There's more work around now. Even in Carrigcapall the work is picking up. And I've said to him he can come back here to the farm while he's looking. Who knows we could get the farm back working again like it was when your granddad was alive?'

Ella breathed in, hardly daring to believe what she was hearing. 'And then maybe I –'

'Shhhh, we said we'd talk about that when I've had a think, petal, there's your mum to think about.'

Ella left it, but held the thought close inside her.

Time passed quite quickly after that. Ella took the dogs for a walk and then came back and ate seven pancakes covered in lemon and cinnamon sugar. By the time it was all cleared away it was three minutes past nine and her granny picked up the phone. She covered the mouthpiece with her hand and told Ella to go outside with the dogs and close the back door. Reluctantly Ella did as she was told and she went and sat out on the kitchen steps, straining to hear what was being said. All she could hear was her granny's voice getting increasingly firm, it was hard to make out any of the words. Ella stood up quietly and carefully pulled down the door handle so she could open the door just a small crack without letting the dogs in. She listened.

'What do you mean, there's nothing you can do? You're the ones who gave the instruction to have the horse picked up, aren't you?'

Ella's heart started thudding.

'Well, I'm not going to leave this, believe me,' she heard her granny say before abruptly replacing the receiver.

Ella pushed open the door and ran in. 'Granny, what did they say?' she said.

Her granny raised her eyebrows. 'Oh, they'll be sorry let me tell you. Stupid woman telling me there's nothing she can do.'

Ella stood and stared at her granny. She had never heard her call anyone stupid before and had never heard her sound so angry.

'Nothing she can do?'

'Those were her exact words. Wagon. Sorry, petal, I shouldn't be saying that, but I can't think of another word right now, she is what she is. It didn't matter what I told her, she kept saying that if the horse is impounded there's nothing she can do and it will cost nine hundred euro to get him back.'

'No-one could afford that much, Granny, and why does Johnny have to pay to get his own horse back?'

Her granny pulled Ella towards her. 'Exactly. And you know that and I know that but someone paid a monthly salary to know these things seems unable to get it. Don't worry. We'll sort her out, even if we have to go in ourselves to get to speak to someone with a little more sense.'

'What'll I tell Johnny?' Ella asked, dreading the answer.

'Tell him the truth, petal, that's all you can do. Tell him we're trying and we'll carry on till we succeed. D'you want to go and see if he's there now?'

Ella nodded. 'I wish I had good news, Granny,' she said in a small voice. 'He's going to be so sad.'

'I know that, petal, but we can't pretend we have good news, can we? That would be cruel. But tell him we won't give up. You'll tell him that?'

Ella nodded and turned to leave, her shoulders drooping with the effort of trying not to show her disappointment.

These People

Johnny reached the field and looked at his phone. It was still so early, only a few minutes after eight. He was going to have a long wait for Ella. He sat down next to the low stone wall and rested his back against it. Within minutes he fell asleep. He woke up with the sun in his eyes and Ella shaking his shoulder.

'Wake up, Johnny, wake up!' He looked at her, confused for a moment as to where he was. 'You fell asleep,' she said.

He rolled his eyes, fully awake now and feeling a bit awkward. 'I can see that, you woke me!' he said. 'What's happening? What did your grandma say?'

Ella looked down at her feet. 'She phoned the council and they said we have to pay nine hundred euro to get the horse back, that's all.'

'I knew it. My da can't pay that. They took him from his field, and they're not allowed to do that.'

'The council?' Ella asked.

'No, the pound. But the council is kind of the boss of them. In a way. They're in charge of loose horses and stuff.

But he wasn't on the road or anywhere like that, so they can't just take him. That's stealing. What if I came to their house and took their dog and then when they want it back I tell them they must pay money for it.'

Ella nodded.

'What can we do?' Johnny asked her.

'Well, she says she'll go to the council about it – it's called the environment department. And Mr Delaney told her you had permission to keep Storm there so she's going to tell them that.'

'Why didn't she tell them that on the phone?'

'She did but they wouldn't listen. They said there's nothing they can do.'

'Ha. Nothing. It's always that. When's she going there? I want to go with her. I'll tell them their business.'

'Today, I think. You can come back with me and we'll talk to her and we can go together, maybe.'

Johnny sat down again, leaning back on the wall. 'She won't mind?'

Ella frowned. 'No, why would she mind?'

'Dunno.'

'She was asking me what your granny's name was.'

'Why?'

'She thinks she might have known her.'

'Annie,' he said quietly.

Ella clapped her hands. 'That's the name she said, she knew her, and now I know you. That's funny, well it's not so much funny as in funny then you laugh like someone's made a joke it's funny odd funny weird funny peculiar because there are so many people living in Carrigcapall and then I meet you and you have a horse and my granny met your granny and my granny had a horse well she had two horses and then your horse gets taken, well that's not funny in any kind of a way that's cruel.' She stopped. 'If you know what I mean?'

Johnny stared at her. 'I s'pose.'

'OK, let's go. Do you need to tell your dad where you're going?'

He shook his head. 'He knows I'm about the place.'

The walk back to the house was faster than usual. Johnny didn't say much. As he walked he swished at the cow parsley with a long stick he'd picked up along the way. Ella gave up trying to talk as all she got was one-word answers. He was probably just thinking of Storm, no wonder he felt like hitting something.

When they got to the back gate she shooed the dogs through first and then beckoned to Johnny to follow her. He looked very uncomfortable. Maybe he was just shy coming to her house.

'My granny's very nice,' she said as they neared the back door. 'She'll make us tea and she always has biscuits if you're hungry.'

He just shook his head. 'I'm all right.'

Ella was hoping her granny wasn't in the secret room as she pushed open the kitchen door. She wasn't sure why she didn't want her to be there but maybe it was because of the sadness that seemed to follow her out of it. Luckily she was sitting at the kitchen table popping peas out of their pods.

'Granny, this is Johnny, it's his horse that's been stolen the one called Storm that I think looks like Black Molly and his grandma is Annie, was Annie, the one you know from way back because I asked him and he told me that was her name isn't that funny? You remember you asked me whether it might be Annie and it is because I asked Johnny and he told me. And it's the same name as our Annie, I wonder could she also be a keepsake of her.'

'It doesn't work like that,' Johnny said. 'It's not about a name.'

'OK, well here we are both of us come to see what we can do about Storm and the council person who said she can do nothing.'

It was as if all the words Ella had not been able to speak on the way from the field had collected in a giant pool in her brain and she'd now pulled the plug on them.

Her granny stood up and went towards Johnny, who was standing just inside the door.

'Hi, Johnny. I'm Ella's granny.' She extended her hand to him and Johnny shook it. 'She talks a lot doesn't she?' she said, smiling as she pointed to Ella.

Johnny nodded, a half grin appearing on his face.

'Sit down. I'll put the kettle on and I'll tell you what I've been doing while you were away.'

Ella pulled out a chair for Johnny and then sat down next to him.

'I phoned that silly woman in the department again and I put the phone on speaker phone and recorded our conversation with my mobile. I thought she would suspect me because the phone kept making buzzing noises but she didn't. So listen to what she said.'

Ella's granny placed her mobile on the table and pressed PLAY on the voice record function.

'Good morning again, ma'am. This is Orla Mackey here. I spoke to you a while ago.'

'Yes, Mrs Mackey, how can I help you?'

'Well, I just wanted to ask you a couple of questions, if that's all right?'

'I told you earlier, if the owner wants the horse back he'll have to pay the release fee. There's no other option.'

'But we have the owner of the field, who will tell you that the horse was in his field legally.'

'The horse was probably on the road; that's why it was taken.'

'No. The horse was in its field when it was taken. I am going to have to take this further, you do know that?'

'Further where? I *am* further, there is nowhere to go past me. And anyway these people leave their horses all over the place, what's so special about this horse?

'These people?'

There was a silence on the other end.

'There's nothing more to be done unless you pay the release fee. And even then I'm not sure because I would need to see proof that the horse is licensed and passported and everything.'

'The horse is chipped; the pound will tell you that. I'll be back to you. What time do your offices close?

'Four p.m. sharp.'

Ella's granny clicked off and started pacing around the kitchen.

'She put the phone down on me; she actually put the phone down. I'm really not about to let her away with it. "These people," she says. How dare she!' She turned to face Johnny, 'You're sure Storm is chipped, Johnny?'

'Yes. Tom Downey does our horses. My da always gets them chipped.'

'What does she mean by "these people", Granny?' Ella asked.

'Travellers. Me. My family,' Johnny said. 'That's who she's talking about.'

Ella looked puzzled for a moment, then frowned. 'She shouldn't speak like that should she, Granny? That's rude.'

'No. Nobody should, petal, but they do. We'll go down to the council offices this afternoon. D'you have a photo of Storm, Johnny?'

'Only an old one when he was a yearling.'

'I have one, Granny. I took one the other day.'

'Good, we'll print that out and start planning. But first, food. I'll put the spuds on. You'll eat with us, Johnny, as long as your mam knows where you are?'

He nodded.

A Bit of a Plan

After dinner Ella's granny got a notebook out that she used to use for the farm accounts. She turned to a blank page. In the middle she stuck the picture of Storm that Ella had printed out. Ella had never seen her granny in this kind of mood before; it was as if she was organising a battle.

'So, here's where we start. Storm was in the field, the gate was closed, he had permission to be there, he had food and water?'

Johnny nodded.

'You checked on him the night before?'

'Yeah, I fed him and filled the water up.'

'The gate when you came there the next day was broken?'

'Yes.'

'Anything else?'

'Tyre tracks in the field.'

'I saw them too, Granny,' Ella said. 'They came through the gate and down to the bottom of the field where Storm was.'

Ella's granny wrote notes on the sheet as they spoke.

'Next we have the person who, according to her, is the boss of Environment. We'll put her here for the moment,' Ella's granny said, as she drew a small stick figure with big hair and stuck her into the corner. 'Then Delaney. He can go here. We need him, as it's his field. He's fond of a scone so we could make some and take them with us when we go to talk to him.'

She drew a pot of jam next to her picture of Delaney.

'Then there's us.' She quickly drew a sketch of a tall woman with a small figure either side of her, 'and finally the pound. You said the pound is in Kiltermon, Johnny?'

'Yes.'

'OK, we must find out where because we might have to go there if we fail with the council'

'You mean drive to Kiltermon?' Ella said.

'Yes. If we need to.'

'I told you,' Ella said, turning to Johnny. 'She'll help us.'

'But what's the plan?' Johnny said, staring at the page now covered in squiggles. 'I don't see a plan.'

'You're right, Johnny. What do you think we should do?' Ella's granny said.

'I don't know. The council won't listen to me. If they don't believe us that the gate was closed they'll just say it was open and Storm was on the road and we can't have him back.' He paused. 'My uncle says we should just go and get the horse, but my da says that's a stupid plan.'

'Your da's right.'

'Well,' he said, 'maybe someone saw them taking Storm.

We can ask around and see if anyone saw them. Because then they can tell the council that he wasn't on the road?'

'Good idea. Maybe some of Delaney's neighbours saw something. I don't know if anyone will remember a number plate but you never know.'

'Or if anyone will say,' Johnny said, 'because some people don't like us having horses.'

Ella turned to him. 'But he's yours. They can't say that.'

'They can say anything. Anyway they took him at night, so no-one would have seen him.'

'Well, they might have done; people stay awake longer in the summer. Who lives near there, Granny?'

'It's Louie Calvert, you remember her, she has that lovely black dog, Charlie?'

'I do! Will you ask her?'

Her granny nodded.

'But if we take pictures of the tyre tracks anyway, that's proof, isn't it?' Ella said.

'Not to the pound man. He'll make up some excuse for that. It was the same with Magic. She was in that field. We never got her back. Or any of the others.'

'Why don't we go and take the photos of the gate and the tyre tracks and everything?' Ella said, not wanting to hear about Magic again. It hurt her head.

'Get close-up pictures if you can. It's lucky we had rain the day before. Otherwise you would have seen nothing.'

'Can we take your phone, Granny? It takes better pictures.'

'Yup. Don't be too long, as we're going to the offices this afternoon and it's already two o'clock.'

Ella called the dogs and she and Johnny set off. Ella hoped the journey back wouldn't be as silent as the one to the farm but, looking at Johnny's face, she could tell it was probably going to be.

Whistling Tunes for Mr Delaney

When they got to the field they found Mr Delaney kneeling down next to the gate trying to fix it. He didn't notice them as he was too busy cursing everything and everybody under and above the sun. They both stood silently until he looked up and saw them.

'Well,' he said, tipping his head to one side.

Ella smiled, a little nervously.

Johnny tipped his own head and replied, 'Well, Mr Delaney.'

Ella had only met him once before, when he had come to help her granny clean out the Aga chimney. He'd not been in a particularly good mood then but her granny told her it was only because he was working. When he wasn't working he was apparently quite nice. Ella found that a little hard to believe.

'So, boy, your horse has gone?'

'They took him.'

'Who took him? You sure he didn't jump the gate? He's a stallion. I warned your dad about keeping a stallion – they can jump anything. Come and hold the gate here, both of you.' He squinted up at Ella. 'You're Pat's young one aren't you? When's he coming back? His ma could do with a hand about the farm. You tell him that from me. Now, both of you hold the end of the gate so it's about six inches off the ground.'

'Can I take a picture first?' Ella said.

'Take the bloody picture – I don't care. Then come and hold the gate.'

Ella took it quickly and then they both ran to where he was pointing and lifted the gate, one either side.

'Whoa, stop just there, no higher.'

'My horse didn't jump the gate,' Johnny said. 'The pound took him. We found the tyre tracks and we're going to take pictures of those too.'

'You'd better be quick about it,' Delaney said. 'There's rain coming. And it could be old tracks from my jeep, could be anything.'

'But the gate was broke,' Johnny said. 'Look.'

'I can see the bloody thing is broken – I'm fixing it,' Delaney muttered. 'You might be right, you might be wrong, who knows, but I don't want trouble that's all I know. I'm too old for it.'

Ella frowned at Johnny, trying to get him to shut up. The more he talked, the angrier Delaney got, and that was the last thing they needed.

'Granny says she's coming over to you later,' Ella said. 'She's been baking.'

Delaney muttered something under his breath that Ella couldn't catch and carried on trying to hammer the hinge back straight. She decided to take her own advice and stop talking.

After about five minutes of a silence punctuated only by the occasional crash of a hammer and more curses from Delaney, Johnny started whistling. It was a tune she didn't know. She glanced at Delaney to see whether it would irritate him further but he seemed to be listening and his frown was no deeper.

'That's nice, boy, what's that tune?'

'It's "The Blue Tar Road",' Johnny said. 'Da sings it when he's doing the horses' feet. It's stuck in my head.'

'Carry on, boy. It stops my head going mad from this bloody gate.'

Johnny looked at Ella and then carried on. Ella's arms started getting sore but she wasn't going to be the first one to ask for a break. Johnny looked unconcerned, whistling away. It seemed this particular song had no end.

'D'you not know another song?' she asked, not sure whether her irritation was with him or with herself as she had never been able to whistle, no matter how many times she'd tried.

'Why don't you whistle a tune then,' Delaney said, lifting his head from his work, 'if you're tired of this one?'

Ella blushed. The last thing she wanted to do was to show Johnny or Mr Delaney her failure of a whistle.

'No, it's not that I'm tired of it. I just wondered if there are different ones.'

Johnny grinned, almost as if he knew. 'I can whistle up of twenty songs, no bother.'

He resumed his whistling, a different tune.

'What name does that one go by?' Delaney asked.

'I don't know the name on this one,' Johnny said. 'I just know the tune.'

'No matter, it's a good tune,' Delaney said, going back to his hammering.

Finally, Ella gave in. 'I need a break, my arms are tired,' she said.

'One more minute, then we're done,' Delaney said. 'Can you hold on for that?'

She nodded and started counting the seconds under her breath.

Finally, on eighty-four, he said to stop.

They both stood there shaking out their arms and then moved out of the way as Delaney swung the gate back to close it again.

'Well?' Johnny said.

'Well what?'

'About my horse.'

'What d'you want me to do?'

'We're going to the council offices this afternoon to speak to them. Can you come with us?'

Delaney scratched his head. 'I'm cutting silage this afternoon. What can I do anyway?'

Ella and Johnny looked at one another.

'You could write us a letter saying the horse was here in the field and you gave him permission to be here,' Ella said.

Delaney wiped his hands on his overalls, picked up his toolbox and headed towards his jeep.

'OK, I'll do that,' he said over his shoulder. 'You'll find it on the seat of my old tractor if I'm not there. The one in the lean-to. Your granny knows it.'

'That's something anyway,' Ella said to Johnny. 'If it's written down there's nothing they can say about it.'

'You don't know them. The only word they seem to know well is no.'

'Well, let's take the photos of the tyre tracks and then head back to the farm.'

They both walked across the stony section towards the hawthorn trees. Johnny quickly found the tracks.

'We have to show that they were taken today because otherwise if they're washed away they could have been taken any day,' he said, looking down at them.

'Granny's phone has a time thing on it, so that's OK.'

They took pictures of everything: the field, the gate, the road, the tracks. Especially the tracks.

Once they'd finished Ella looked at the time. 'It's getting late, we should head back now.'

Johnny didn't reply. He just started whistling again. Ella looked across at him. Maybe she could get him to teach her how to whistle so that when her dad came back she could surprise him with it. First, though, she would have to get over the fact of having to admit to Johnny that she couldn't whistle. Maybe she'd ask him another day.

Too Many Horses Anyway

When they got back to the house they found Ella's granny on the phone again. She put it down as they came in.

'That was Delaney. He says we can pick up his statement. It's on the seat of his Ferguson 135. So, if you're ready, we'll go now. It's almost three so we'll make it in time. Anyone need the loo, go now.'

'Granny!' Ella said, mortified.

'Sorry, petal,' her granny said, not looking the least bit sorry, 'just in case.'

Johnny looked down at the ground and shook his head.

'Right so, we'll go.'

When they got to the car Ella debated with herself about where to sit. She didn't want to sit in the front and leave Johnny sitting by himself, but she didn't want him to get the front seat either. She opened the back door.

'We'll both sit in the back, Granny,' she said. 'It's easier.'

Her granny made no comment but Ella could see she wanted to.

They reached Delaney's and Ella jumped out to get the paper that was sitting, squished under a rock, on the tractor seat. She brushed off the soil and tried to straighten it out, then jumped back into the car.

She read it out.

'"I, Jimmy Delaney, am the owner of the field which sits on the left hand side of the Kilinore road about two mile from town. I gave permission to Mr John Joyce to keep horses in this field. He has permission for 2016 and 2017." Signed Jimmy Delaney. His signature is just a squiggle, you can't even make out that it's a name. Does that matter?'

'Not at all – it's a signature. It only has to look like all the other times he's signed something. Put it on the front seat, petal, and we'll head.'

Once they'd parked the car in a space behind the council offices, Ella started to feel nervous. She looked at Johnny and could see he was feeling exactly the same.

'Granny, do we have to come in with you to see whoever you're seeing?'

'No. But you can come into the offices and wait in the waiting area.'

Ella's granny walked up to the reception desk. 'I'm here to see anyone from the Environment section, please.'

'You have an appointment?'

'No.'

'You'll have to make an appointment.'

He picked up the phone and spoke into it for a few minutes. Neither Ella nor Johnny could hear what he was saying.

He put the phone down and looked up. 'You can see Mr Reilly on Tuesday next week.'

'No I can't, as by then it'll be too late. This is an urgent matter and I need to see someone today. I don't care who I see – Bill or Tommy or John or Jane, anyone.'

He frowned. 'There's no Bill or Tommy or John working in the department. Are you sure it's Environment you want?'

'I know, I know, they're only examples. You know, like Tom, Dick or Harry. I'm just saying I'll see anyone, it's an emergency. I'll wait here till you let me through.'

The man behind the desk started to look flustered.

'All right. Just go through those double doors and you can ask reception at Environment.'

Granny turned to go, winking at the two of them as she left. The man on reception looked very relieved to be rid of her. Ella didn't blame him – her granny was quite scary when she wanted something done.

They sat waiting there, neither of them saying a word, for what seemed like months.

Johnny finally turned to Ella. 'If this all fails, we have to have a plan. I can't let them kill him. I won't.'

'What kind of a plan? Like your uncle's plan?' Ella said nervously.

He shook his head. 'No. But maybe if we get the story in the paper or on the radio or something. We could put pictures up of him and you could write the story about him.'

'We could,' Ella said hesitantly. 'I've never done anything with the papers before.'

'Their offices are in town. I know where they are. We could run there now while your grandma is busy?'

Ella shook her head. 'No. What if she comes out and then we've gone? She'd be upset.'

As she was speaking the doors swung open and her granny came through. From the look on her face it had not gone well.

'Come on, lads, we'll talk in the car,' she said.

Johnny felt his heart sinking as they walked towards the car in silence. Once they were inside it Ella's granny let out a long sigh.

'Damn. I forgot to get the code for the gate to get out and I'm not paying another cent towards this place. Johnny, would you be a pet and run and ask the man at the desk for the code?'

It was the last thing in the world Johnny felt like doing but he got out of the car and started running towards the building.

'Granny,' Ella said, 'what happened?'

'Nothing. Exactly nothing. They just sat there when I eventually got to see them and said "there's nothing we can do. You have no proof the horse wasn't out on the road and the people who picked the horse up said he was, so that's the end of it. If the owner wants to reclaim the horse they can pay us the nine hundred and then they can go down and fetch the horse." It didn't matter what I said, it didn't matter that I showed them Delaney's letter, or the picture of the broken gate. Nothing. I don't know what to tell Johnny.'

Ella looked out of the window and saw Johnny running back.

'Tell him you're coming back tomorrow. You didn't tell them about the tracks, did you?'

Her granny smiled suddenly. 'No! How could I have forgotten those? I can bring them in tomorrow. I won't go back in now as they're really irritated with me, which doesn't help.'

Johnny opened the door. '9293 is the code. And,' he said, sitting forward, 'I heard them talking when I came back next to the window.'

'Who?'

'I don't know. I couldn't see their faces, but one woman was asking if there was perhaps a mistake and your man said it didn't matter because there's too many horses anyway.'

'You're sure?' Ella's granny said. 'Did she have a kind of high-pitched voice?'

'Squeaky, like?'

'Yes.'

He nodded.

'Brilliant. If we need to, we'll use that. I know who she is and I think I know who he is.'

'So what did they say when you were in?' Johnny said as they drove off.

'I'll tell you as we drive and we'll drop you off at home.'

A Spider-free Zone

Ella headed to bed early that night but it was hot and the shadows on her ceiling had started to form unfamiliar shapes. This probably happened when she was asleep every other night, she thought, so if she went to sleep she wouldn't see them any more. She knew that most of the shadows came from cobwebs that her granny refused to get rid of because she said, 'Spiders are our friends they get rid of the flies.' Which was easy for her granny to say because she actually liked them. Ella didn't. If she was given a choice, and she wasn't, of having ten flies in her room or one small spider she would go for the flies any day. It was one of the very small downsides of coming down to live here. But if she was here all the time and this became her very own room then there was no reason that she couldn't have this room as a spider-free zone.

She lay in the dark and closed her eyes. Tomorrow couldn't come fast enough. Surely if her granny went in to the council again with the photos of the tyre tracks and the evidence of what Johnny heard, then that would be that. She didn't want to see Johnny's face fall as it had done when Granny had told him some of what had been said in the offices. All he'd said, before they dropped him off, was, 'I told you, they won't believe us. And I had my papers and all.'

Granny had said, in her brisk voice that Ella knew she kept for times when she needed to persuade herself that things were going to be OK, 'We'll sort them out, Johnny, I promise you. We'll pick you up here tomorrow at nine o'clock sharp.'

Johnny nodded. 'Thanks,' he said, so quietly that it was only Ella who heard him.

Her granny woke her up at eight. 'Come down for breakfast, petal; then we'll go and fetch Johnny, see if we can cheer him up today.'

'And when all this is over and Storm is safe can we talk about the spiders, Granny?' Ella said.

Her granny laughed. 'Ella, Ella, poor little spiders never hurt anyone.'

Ella peeped over the top of her duvet. 'No, but I don't want to share my bedroom with them, Granny.'

Her granny looked at her. 'OK, petal, we'll get the ones in your room to move house. I won't kill them, mind you, just move them. That's a promise. Once we've sorted Storm out we'll move on to the spiders. You can wait till then?'

Ella moved her whole head out. 'I can, I can! I'll get up now.'

'And you're right in a way, petal, to be scared of spiders. We all, way back when, came from Africa. And the spiders in Africa are definitely things to be afraid of. We probably have a little memory tucked away in our heads of that time, even though we don't know it.'

She looked at her granny and there above her head was a jumble of laughter and a small hairy spider. Ella shuddered involuntarily and her granny smiled sideways at her before heading downstairs.

'I phoned Louie by the way, petal,' she said when Ella came into the kitchen, 'and she said she heard what she thought was a truck on that night stopping outside the field. At about half eleven. She's happy to tell the council and the pound but I'm not sure it's enough. She was wondering where Storm had gone as she used to bring him carrots.

'It helps anyway, doesn't it?'

'Everything helps, no matter how small.'

Ella hoped that was true.

After breakfast she took the dogs for a short walk before they left. Her granny had printed the photos out and put them into a folder with the licence papers that Johnny had given them and they set off in the car. As they reached Johnny's place Ella turned to her.

'Thank you about the spiders, Granny, and I don't want you to kill them I just don't want them in my bedroom in case they fall down from the ceiling while I'm sleeping and run about on my face it's not that I hate them or anything or wish there weren't any spiders I know there have to be but I wish they'd stay away from me that's all. And thank you for agreeing to help us with this.'

She watched as her granny tried not to laugh, raising her eyebrows with the effort of it.

'That's OK, petal.'

Johnny opened the car door and jumped in.

'Morning, Johnny,' her granny said. 'We were just talking about spiders. How do you feel about them?'

He shrugged. 'Well, they're everywhere, so I'm not bothered getting fussed about them. They're just like flies or something, they won't hurt me.'

Ella wished her granny hadn't asked him his opinion, especially as he answered as if they were nothing. She looked across at her and thought she saw a small bubble of regret sitting on her granny's shoulder. She felt just a little mollified by that.

Twenty-four Hours in a Day

Once again Johnny and Ella found themselves sitting in the hallway of the council offices while Ella's granny went in to speak to the officials. Johnny put his hands on the edge of the seat, stared at the floor and swung his legs.

'Can we go now down to the newspaper office? It'll take five minutes.'

Ella started to reply but as she did the doors opened and her granny emerged with another woman and pointed towards them.

'Johnny,' she called, 'would you mind coming here for a minute, pet?'

Johnny frowned and got to his feet, quickly followed by Ella.

'No, petal, not you, you wait there.'

Johnny walked over and stood in front of the two women.

'Mrs Dalton just wants to ask you a few questions about Storm, Johnny,' Ella's granny said, touching him lightly on his shoulder.

'Hi, Johnny.'

'Well,' he said, wishing she would stop staring and get on with whatever she was going to ask him.

'This is your horse?'

'No. He's my da's horse. I look after him. He's a keepsake of my grandma.'

The woman stared at him. 'A keepsake?'

'A memory of his granny,' Ella's granny said.

The woman shook her head. 'And he stays in that field, and he never got out of that field?'

'Yes – no,' he said.

'Yes or no?'

'Yes he stays in the field and no he never got out of it.'

'And these papers – they belong to him not to some other horse?'

Ella's granny answered before he could. 'You don't need Johnny to answer that, because at the pound they can scan the chip in the horse's neck and see if it's the same horse. You know that.'

The woman nodded and carried on.

'Do you pay rent to Mr Delaney?'

Johnny shook his head.

'No? So he lets you have the land for free?'

'No. My da pays the rent.'

'I think we're done here,' Ella's granny said, frowning at the woman. 'Johnny, you go and sit down with Ella. I'll see you in a minute.'

With that she disappeared back inside with Mrs Dalton.

'What did she want?' Ella asked. 'I could barely hear a word.'

'She was just asking me about Storm: did he always stay in the field, did he jump out? I don't know how she can think he opens gates, she looked like she didn't believe me. Is he a different horse or something? Like, did some other horse have that licence? I don't know why she wanted to ask me anything because your granny told her already, it's as if she was trying to trick me. She asked me is he my horse but I'm not sixteen so I can't own a horse so I told her he's my da's horse. And it's true – the licence is in his name.'

'Johnny, I've been thinking,' Ella said, a look of panic on her face, 'what if they took him in the night, but they count that as a full day? If they do then we've only got till tomorrow,' Ella said, 'and what if they say no, if that woman says no again, then what are we going to do?'

Johnny looked at her, his face mirroring hers. 'What? But you can't count a night as a day. If they do, does that mean tomorrow they can kill him?'

Ella sat and counted off the days on her fingers. 'So is day one the day they take him?'

Johnny nodded.

'Day two you found the gate open. And then we made a plan with Granny.'

'Day three we went to the council, the first time.'

And day four is today and here we are at the council again.' Ella looked down at her hand, only her thumb was left. 'Tomorrow is day five.'

She looked up. 'Are you sure they count the days from

the time they fetch him? They can't count that as a full day because if it's in the night then there's only a few hours left and if it's near midnight they picked him up then that's almost the next day so it would be cheating to call it one day when it wasn't, because one day can't be half an hour long unless they're using American time and that could be eight hours behind us so that could be twelve hours but they can't use that time because we don't live in America and especially the council can't use that time because they're like the government.' She got up. 'I'm going to get Granny to ask them.'

She started running towards the double doors and pushed them open. 'Granny, Granny. Where are you?'

Ella stopped and looked around. To her left was a glass-fronted reception window. She ran to it and a woman looked up from her desk. 'Can I help you, dear?' she said.

'I'm looking for my granny. She's got grey hair and she's not too tall except she thinks she is and she's called Mrs Mackey and she's here with Mrs Walton.'

'Mrs Dalton?' the woman replied, smiling.

'Yes, that's the one, I need to speak to her to ask her about whether the five days starts four days ago or three days ago because you see that depends on how you count a day and we think, me and Johnny, that you can't count a day as a day if it only has a few hours in it or even just one hour or even minutes.'

'Um, a day is twenty-four hours so you're right there but sometimes –' she shook her head. 'I think you'd better check this with Mrs Dalton as I am not sure what it's in connection with.' She picked up the phone and pressed a couple of numbers, 'Jane? I have a little girl here. I think her granny is with you. She wants to check something with you.'

She put the phone down. 'They'll be out in a minute. She asked if you would wait in the waiting area.'

Ella's shoulders slumped. 'OK, but you agree with me?'

'About?'

'About how long a day is?'

'Yes. I agree with that, generally, but sometimes I suppose a day could be twelve hours if you're talking about day time not night time, if you see what I mean?'

Ella nodded. 'That's my worry,' she said as she left and pushed back through the glass doors.

A Little Bit of Good

Johnny and Ella sat in complete silence while they waited, all thoughts of the newspaper gone as they both felt time running away from them. Ella's thoughts were not quiet, though, because Storm was high-stepping through them, his neck arched and his nostrils flaring. She couldn't see what Johnny's thoughts were. But, she thought, if Storm had taken over her whole brain and she'd only known him a few days, how much worse could it be in the head of someone who'd loved him every day since he was born?

Ella was the first one to break the silence. 'Did you say they use a cattle trailer to take them to Kiltermon?'

Johnny nodded. 'Once they put ten mares into the trailer, they were squashed together and four of the mares were in foal so we don't know what happened to them. They could have foaled in the trailer and then the foal could have got killed.'

'Johnny, that's awful. D'you think there were other ones taken with Storm?'

'I don't know. I didn't hear of any. None around us, maybe somewhere else.'

'Why don't they use a horsebox? Or one of those big lorries for horses? Isn't that how you're supposed to move a horse around?'

Before Johnny could answer, the doors opened and her granny appeared. Ella looked at her anxiously. The cloud of thoughts above her head was like a swarm of angry bees, dark and buzzing. They both jumped up.

'What did she say?' asked Johnny.

'Let's get out of here and I'll tell you when we're in the car,' she said, shepherding them to the door. 'Let's go.'

Johnny knew that the news wasn't good. He didn't need to be able to see her thoughts. He knew if it had been good news she would have come straight out to them and told them.

Once they were all in the car, Ella's granny turned sideways in her seat so she could see them both.

'I don't know what to do. It doesn't matter what I say – she keeps telling me that there's nothing she can do as I have no proof that the horse was taken out of the field. She phoned the pound when I was in her office and they told her the horse was out on the road. I've shown her the pictures of the tyre tracks and the broken gate but she says that proves nothing.'

'We need to match the tyre tracks, Granny, that's all,' Ella said. 'That's one hundred per cent proof. What if we call the pound and pretend that there's horses somewhere illegally they need to pick up? Then we can wait in the field for them and see if they match.'

'Well, we could do that, petal, except that would be lying and I'm not going to lie.'

'But, Granny, they're lying so it would just be one lie cancelling out another lie.'

'Doesn't work like that, Ella; two lies are two lies. You add them, you don't take one away from another. No. I'm not doing that. We have to find another way.'

'Well,' Ella said, looking sideways at Johnny, 'we could lie. Me and Johnny. I don't mind lying if it means that Storm won't be killed.'

Johnny nodded.

'And,' Ella continued, 'if you look at it it's not really a lie; it's a trick, and everyone plays tricks.'

'No. That's all, just no,' her granny said. 'We'll fix it without that.'

She sat tapping her fingers on the steering wheel till the noise of them started to bore right into Johnny's brain. 'We can ask them,' he said suddenly, 'to compare the tracks with their trailer. The pattern, like?'

Ella's granny turned to face him. 'Brilliant! That's exactly what we'll do, Johnny. They can't refuse that. I think there's even something where you can compare soil, because each place has its own soil. We could say we'll get a lawyer to do that if they don't let us.' She paused. 'Maybe we can ask your one, Johnny, the one you heard saying it was a mistake, or maybe a mistake? The one with the squeaky voice?'

He nodded.

'We can ask her permission to go down. We can take the horsebox and fetch Storm all at the one time,' Ella said. 'And we can tell her we heard what the man said about too many horses.'

'We can say that, because that's the truth. Your dad has a horsebox, Johnny?' Ella's granny asked.

'Yeah.'

'Good. We can borrow that. My car has a hitch we can use.'

'But isn't she the same one who keeps telling you she can't do anything?' Ella asked.

'She is.'

'And you called her a wagon, Granny, and she was rude about Johnny.'

'I know. But I have a feeling she might be thinking about it,' she said, 'And this way there are no lies or tricks involved. We need to get back inside to see her quickly.' She looked at Johnny. 'Come on, smile, this is going to work. If we go down early tomorrow morning we can be home by dinnertime with Storm.'

Johnny looked unconvinced, as did Ella.

'But what if tomorrow is day five, Granny? It could be, we worked it out. It might be too late.'

'And they're not going to say yes. She doesn't even believe the papers are for the same horse, how's she going to say yes?' Johnny said, shrugging his shoulders. 'But if she does, then my da can take us down to fetch Storm if you want.'

'We'll talk about that later.' Ella's granny pushed open

the doors and then pointed to the seats they had only just vacated. 'Wait here. I'm going in to see her.'

'This might work, Johnny,' Ella whispered once her granny had gone.

'I can't believe that now,' he said, his tired head sunk into his shoulders. 'I think I might never ever see him again.'

'I'm just …' Ella said, 'I s'pose I'm just trying to believe it.'

As time passed she started to feel her spirits dropping until her granny came bursting through the glass doors again.

'They've agreed! Mrs Dalton herself said she will come down, but in her own car, tomorrow morning and compare the photo of the tracks with the actual tyre. I told her we could get soil tested as well, even though I'm not sure how.'

Johnny leapt to his feet. 'What?'

Ella ran to her granny and started hugging her. 'You sure, Granny?'

'Yes, petal. And Mrs Dalton even seemed a bit pleased to be able to help us. Maybe she felt bad. She's just following the rules really so we can't blame her.'

Ella and Johnny looked at one another and grinned. 'That's just you always looking for the good in a person, Granny, even if that good is really really tiny compared to all the bad. You always say we have to look for the good. You even told me I had to do that with my fourth-class teacher and that was very hard.'

'Well, whatever it is, she's the one who's giving us this chance, so let's be thankful for that. Now, let's go before anyone changes their mind.

Cousins and Pups

'We'll drop you at home, Johnny, if you want,' Ella's granny said once they were back in the car.

'It's OK. You can drop me at the garage near the roundabout. I'll walk home.'

'I was thinking we might go by your house this evening. Just to see if your dad wants to go down,' she said.

'You want to go down, don't you, Granny?' Ella wanted her granny to do the driving as that meant she could go too.

'I do, petal. You forget I've never seen Storm. But I also want to check that the trailer fits my hitch. We need to leave early so we'll check this evening that everything is ready.'

'OK, you can bring me home then,' Johnny said quietly.

'Good, and besides, I'd very much like to chat with your dad.'

Ella was quite sure that Johnny flinched at that. He'd probably already realised that there was no knowing what Ella's granny might say next

After what seemed to Ella like a long roundabout route they eventually reached Johnny's place. Her granny drove in slowly and pulled to a stop. Within seconds a crowd of small children surrounded the car.

'Are these all your brothers and sisters, Johnny?' Ella said, realising as it came out what a ridiculous question it was, as most of them were the same height as each other.

'Some of them are,' he said, letting her off with it. 'Most of them are my cousins but we all live on the site here.'

'I wish I had even one brother or sister, or two. You're so lucky. How many actual brothers and sisters do you have?

'Nine.'

'Wow, that's like you, Granny, almost – you had seven didn't you?'

'I did, petal.'

'There's my da. You can come and meet him,' Johnny said, pointing to a small paddock to the side of the house, 'and then you can come and see my pups. They're only two weeks old.'

They walked over towards Johnny's father, who was filling a water bucket in the paddock. Ella's granny went forward. 'Hello, I'm Orla Mackey,' she said.

'This is the lady I was telling you about. She knew Grandma Annie way back.'

His father wiped his hands on his jeans and smiled. 'Any friend of my ma is welcome here. I'm John Joyce.'

'She was a lovely woman. She used to sell me pots and come in for a cup of tea. I'm very sorry for your loss,' Ella's granny said.

'Too soon she went. She didn't get to see my youngest boy.'

'Tell him about the council lady,' Johnny interrupted.

'Well, the council said we can go and fetch him if we can prove that the tyres in the field are the same as the vehicle belonging to the pound. I think they must have realised they made a mistake because of Delaney's letter and the papers, so they're trying to find a way out of it. We will need a box tomorrow. Johnny says you have one. I don't mind driving down with it.'

Johnny's da shaded his eyes from the sun and looked at Ella's granny. 'You believe them? They said you can take him without paying the fee?'

'I think I believe them, and it's worth a try,' she said.

'They'll find some other excuse. Even if the tyre tracks match, they'll come up with something. Did you talk to Delaney?'

'I did, and he gave me a letter saying the horse was allowed in the field, so that part's OK.'

'You can take the box. Johnny, you and Mikey clean it out quickly then we'll hitch it up.' He turned towards Ella's granny. 'Who were you talking to in the council?'

'Mrs Dalton.'

He frowned. 'I don't know her. She must be new.'

'She might be. At first she just kept telling us there was nothing she could do, but maybe it's because she's scared to do anything that's not in the rules.'

'Maybe. Can you handle the horse if you get him?'

'I can, and I'll have Johnny with me so he can load him.'

'And you can pull a box?'

She nodded. 'I used to have horses, until –' She stopped herself. 'Well, I used to have them, so it'll be fine.'

'Ella,' Johnny called, 'come and see the pups.'

Ella went towards a wooden shed behind the houses and Johnny opened the door. Inside there were four of the smallest puppies Ella had ever seen, lying on a bed of straw with their mum.

'They're whippets!' she said.

'Yes. The mother's mine, and all four puppies are girls. Here,' he said, picking one up and handing it to her, 'you can hold one. She doesn't mind.'

Ella held the pup gently and nuzzled her face into its soft fur. It was a pale golden colour with dark tips on its ears.

'You can come and see them any time you want, after we get Storm back,' he said.

'Ella, Johnny, let's go,' her granny called. 'The box is hitched.'

'Johnny,' she said, as they ran back towards her, 'we'll pick you up at about six. That OK?'

Johnny just nodded, the reality of it only starting to sink in.

Dandelion and May

'Granny, I wish you'd seen those puppies. They're the sweetest little things, baby whippets. Maybe when they grow up …' Ella said once they were back in the car.

'I know what you're going to say, petal, and we can't just get every animal you see, we'd be overrun. And little puppies grow very fast.'

'I know, I know, but they're beautiful. They're like mini-Annies. She'd like one because then she could pretend it was her puppy and she's never been a mum so that'd be good and Grouse could think he was the dad and they'd be a happy family and Old Greg when he's around could be like a visiting uncle or something and if it got cold in the winter it could come and sleep in my bed if I was living here by then which I might be, you never know.'

'You never know is right. Here we are anyway, and here are the hounds. I'll park this with the box facing outwards ready to go in the morning. Johnny's da gave me some hay for the net and a bucket of nuts to help us get him in the box.'

Ella grinned. 'D'you think it's going to work? Like, really work?'

'Let's hope so, petal. Nothing's definite.'

'But you said …'

'I know what I said, but you can never be one hundred per cent about anything. Apart from the fact that the sun will rise and then it'll set again.'

Ella got out of the car, frowning. There was so little time left, and even if they went down there the pound could still say no. She remembered Johnny saying that it had happened with their other horse. She'd have to speak to Johnny without her granny hearing so that between them they could come up with a plan if the tyre track thing didn't work.

After tea Ella sat in the kitchen for a while playing rummy with her granny. Her granny seemed distracted or else she was just letting Ella win each and every game. She didn't do that usually. It was getting closer to bed time when her granny turned to her.

'I'm not going to tell you a story tonight but I think I'll tell you something I've been wanting to tell you for a while. It's sad, which is why I haven't told it to you before. D'you mind if it's a bit sad, petal?'

Ella held her breath as she saw uncertainty in her granny's thoughts, wobbling softly above her head. She shook her head. 'I prefer happy stories, but I don't mind sad. Just not all the time.'

'OK. So, come on, we'll go in here,' her granny said, pointing to the locked door of the secret room.

'There?' Ella said, shocked into speaking.

'Yes. I know you've never been in there and d'you know your dad hasn't been in there either. Not since he was very young. But we'll go in there today.'

Ella got up and Annie and Grouse pricked up their ears watching her.

'Can they come too?'

'Yes, petal, of course.'

Granny led the way. She unlocked the door and opened it. Ella, Grouse and Annie followed her in. Ella stood and stared. She had often imagined what was in here but nothing she'd imagined came close to this. In the far corner of the room was a bed covered with a patchwork quilt. Three teddy bears sat up against the pillow – a dark brown one with a small blue jacket on, a pale brown one and a tiny white one with a black nose propped up in between them. In the opposite corner was a table with a doll's house on it. The house was wooden. The windows were painted white and the door bright yellow.

In the centre of the room on a pale green carpet was a large armchair covered in a multi-coloured crocheted blanket. In front of it was a small footstool. Ella just stood and stared. Her granny said nothing until Ella turned to her, confused.

'I know, petal, it's probably not what you expected. But this is what I'm going to tell you about.' She went and sat down in the chair and leaned forward to pat the footstool. 'You come and sit here and the dogs can sit next to you.

They're used to this room as they always come with me when I'm in here.'

Ella came and sat down and looked up at her granny, a million questions running around her head. She was a little relieved to see that the wobbling thoughts had calmed down a little.

'This room, petal, is like my memory box, a place where I keep some of the memories that I've never been able to share with anyone. You see, apart from your dad,' she paused and took a deep breath – 'I had another child, a little girl called May. She was six years older than him.'

'Dad has a sister?' Ella said, incredulous.

'Wait, petal, be patient, I'll tell you. I named her after the flower of the hawthorn tree, you know the one just outside the back door? In spring it's covered in beautiful white flowers. They're called May blossom.'

Ella frowned. 'Yes, but –'

Her granny continued, ignoring the interruption. 'She was a lovely little girl, full of life, You remind me a little bit of her some days. You know how you chatter with no full stops in between or anything? I remember her doing that. Especially when she'd get up and come into our bedroom to wake us up.'

Her granny smiled, but it wasn't her usual smile. It was a smile, Ella could see, that cost her just a little more effort than usual.

'She was a very busy child, like your dad. They loved each other a lot, even though she was a good few years older than him. May was so excited when I came home from the hospital with him, and for the first few weeks she used to sit by his cradle in the kitchen just watching him sleep.

'But, apart from her baby brother, what May loved most were animals. All animals, but horses were definitely her favourite. From as soon as she could walk she would follow me whenever I had to feed the horses. Both Giant and Black Molly were getting quite old by then but they were happy and well. She had no fear, despite the fact that she was so tiny and they were so huge.

'She first started learning to ride when she was five years old. It was a bit soon but I was running out of ways to say no to her. Up until then I had allowed her to sit up on Black Molly with me. Your granddad would hand her up to me once I'd mounted and then he would lead us around the field. I never did it on my own. He always had to be there. There was something about sitting on a horse that just settled May. If she had been feeling restless or irritable and we went out and put her up on Black Molly with me, all her troubles seemed to melt away. Not that she often had troubles but whichever little ones she did have disappeared. This is a photo your granddad took of her and me on Black Molly.'

She handed Ella a faded colour photograph in a wooden frame. Ella stared at it. Black Molly had turned her head to the camera and on top of her was her granny and a small girl, who looked vaguely familiar to her. Her hair was black and curly, tied back with a blue ribbon and she was leaning back against Ella's granny who had her held tightly around the waist.

Ella looked up at her granny. In that instant she knew. She knew why her granny had said this was going to be sad – the little girl in the picture, with the curly black hair, was the reason. She almost didn't want to hear the rest of it. And as often happened between the two of them, her granny could see that Ella knew. Neither of them spoke for a moment; then her granny carried on.

'Once May had learned to ride there was no stopping her, she was a natural, I hardly had to teach her anything. And she was so kind to the horses. By the time she was seven, and your dad was just one year old, I was letting her ride without a lead rein. We had a head collar we used instead of a bridle. Now you can get bitless bridles but we didn't have them then so we used a leather head collar. Black Molly was used to it, she'd never known anything else, so she'd listen to your legs and your voice. Every chance May got she'd be out to the field grooming the two horses, then calling me to watch her as she rode Black Molly.

'As time passed she started asking me if she could ride Giant. At first I didn't let her. He was even taller than his mother – he stood at nearly seventeen hands, and I'd been the only one to ride him so far. But he was very gentle, so, as May got better at riding, I decided to let her try him. They were perfect together Ella. It was as if he knew he had a precious little girl on his back. He did everything right and her riding improved day by day. By the time she was eight she was a far better rider than I ever was, and I'd been riding my whole life.

Ella breathed in, her heart beating hard in her chest. Her

granny continued, her voice different to when she told the other stories. Quieter. Ella had to listen really hard to hear all the words.

'One day we decided to go for a ride out of the paddock and take the horses to the rath field. Your granddad looked after your dad at the house. We packed a little picnic of ginger biscuits and a jam roll and I carried that in a rucksack on my back. We set off. As you know, petal, it's not that far to the rath field – you walk that most days – but for May it was a big adventure. She was so excited, she chatted to Giant the whole way there. We trotted down the lane and once we got to the rath field we cantered to the top of the hill, then dismounted so we could have our little picnic. We let the horses loose so they could graze a little on the fresh grass. I remember us both lying back at the top of the small hill watching the clouds. They seemed to be moving very quickly, as if they were chasing one another across the sky. I remember May saying to me that day, "I'm the happiest girl in the whole world today. I don't think that there's any girl in any corner of the earth who is happier than me." Isn't that lovely, petal?'

Ella nodded, although she didn't think it especially lovely if what she suspected was true.

'Anyway we then got back on. I always had to give her a leg up as she was too short, and then I did a running mount onto Black Molly. She was so used to me that she wouldn't move till I was safely up on her back. We set off again. A small breeze had started but nothing to worry about. As we reached the gate from the rath field into the triangle field a young hare jumped out of the ditch and stood up, as hares do, right in front of Giant. He got a terrible fright and did something that he'd never done before. He reared up on his hind legs and May went flying off his back.'

Her granny sat perfectly still, tears streaming down her face.

'Our little May didn't survive the fall. The doctor said she felt nothing, she died instantly. It's hard to be glad about anything but I'm glad she felt nothing. I have lain awake for so many nights worrying about whether she did, but I know the doctor wouldn't have lied to me. He wasn't like that.' She released her hold on Ella's hand a little and her shoulders relaxed. 'You know, petal, I've been thinking for ages about whether to tell you and I'm relieved I did. I don't want May to be a secret in the house any more. Your dad was just two when it happened. In a way he was too young to know a lot about it. He knew she was no longer there and I didn't want to hurt him more by talking about her. Your grandfather, whom you never knew, was lost after it happened. Completely lost.'

Ella didn't know what to say, but it didn't matter. Even though her granny was speaking, Ella could see she was just lost in that time, so long ago. She might not even have heard anything Ella said.

'I put all her things in this room so they could be close to me during the day. At first I used to come into it every evening and sit in it after your dad had gone to sleep. That carried on for many years. It was as if there was a little part of her in here. It's still like that. I can feel what she was like when I come in here. But I only talked to myself about her, never to your dad and never to your grandfather. I don't know if I did the right thing because it's as if I was stealing away your dad's memory of her. But I didn't know what else to do. She'd gone, and the pain in my heart was so sharp I couldn't think straight. I think in a way, petal, I became a little mad with the grief of it. But now, having you here and watching you grow up, it seemed like the right time to tell you. I chat to her, you know, when I come in here.'

Ella did know, as she had heard the mumblings through the closed door.

'Sometimes I make myself a cup of tea and I come and sit in the armchair just like I'm doing now, and I talk to her. About everything. She knows all about you and she knows you might one day come here and live with us and I think, wherever she is, she'd be very happy about that.'

The two of them sat in silence for a while, Ella's thoughts twirling and tumbling. Her granny leaned down and hugged her.

'Sorry, petal. Maybe I shouldn't even have told you. But the reason I started thinking about telling you was because of Johnny remembering his grandma. He remembers her out loud, doesn't he? And maybe that's best.'

'It's OK, Granny. I see now,' Ella said, looking around the room.

'See what, petal?'

'Why you never wanted me to ride,' Ella said in a quiet voice.

Her granny closed her eyes and scrunched up her face. 'And that was wrong, petal. I can't do that for ever, and I won't. I promise you. It will change now'

Ella didn't say anything for a while but then she stood up and wandered over to the little bed. 'These are like your keepsakes of her, of May? This whole room is like that.'

Her granny nodded. 'It is.'

'Should I have a keepsake of her as well?' Ella said, 'Just a small thing because I didn't know her but if she was alive she would have been my aunt.'

'She would. What about him?' her granny said, pointing to the dark brown teddy with the blue jacket. 'He was her favourite. He's called Dandelion.'

Ella got up and went over to the small bed. She picked up the teddy, hugging him to her. 'He might like a new owner,' she said, sniffing him. 'He smells a bit like … something old … if you know what I mean?'

'I do, petal.'

Her granny sat perfectly still on the chair and Ella could see nothing floating above her head. No darkness. No light. Ella looked at her, not quite sure what to do.

'Granny?'

Her granny started. 'Yes, petal, sorry. Away with the fairies I am.' She shook herself and stood up. 'Now, we have a long day tomorrow, so a hot drink and then to bed.' She bent down to kiss Ella's head. 'I'm glad I've told you about my May. And I'm never going to lock this door again. I'll just let her be a part of us in her own way, not a hidden way. Out loud like Johnny and Storm and old Annie Joyce.'

Ella nodded, a small pain in her heart for the sadness she could see still clouding her granny's eyes.

That night she lay in bed, holding Dandelion close to her, and within minutes her eyelids drooped and she fell into a deep sleep.

The Longest Journey

Johnny slept deeper that night than he had since Storm had been taken. It wasn't that he fully believed yet that they would get him back – it was just exhaustion.

'My brain is tired,' he said to his da before he headed to bed. 'It's like it ran out of space for thinking.'

'Go on with you and your brain. Get some sleep,' his da said, 'and we'll see tomorrow what happens. I bought a padlock today for the gate at Delaney's. That might slow them down next time they try anything.'

Johnny didn't answer, as he couldn't imagine ever letting Storm out of his sight if they got him back.

In the morning when he woke up a light drizzle of rain was falling and everything looked dull and grey outside the window.

Mikey, who slept in the bed next to him, turned over and said, 'D'you really think you'll get him back from the pound?'

Johnny shrugged. 'Maybe, but maybe not. They never

gave us a horse back yet. Ella's granny thinks we'll get him but she's a bit cracked.'

'Maybe she just likes horses?'

'That's what Ella says, but I dunno.'

'If you don't get him back, what will Grandma think?' Mikey blessed himself as he said it.

Johnny looked up to the ceiling. 'Don't say that, Mikey. I don't want to think about it.'

Just then they heard a car horn. Johnny stood and looked out of the window. Ella and her granny were there with the horsebox. He pulled on his track pants and rummaged under the bed for his shoes.

'Go and tell them I'm coming,' he yelled at Mikey. 'They're way too early.' Mikey ran outside and Johnny went into the kitchen. He thought for a minute about eating but his stomach was in knots of nerves, so he just headed out through the back door and ran to the car.

He jumped in, waved to Mikey, then turned to Ella. 'It's half past five. Why are you so early? You said six o'clock.'

'Granny wants to drive very slowly,' Ella said, seemingly unperturbed by his outburst. 'She hasn't pulled a trailer in years. And anyway, it's better to be early.'

'Ella's been awake since half past four, Johnny,' her granny said, 'and I was tired of watching her watching the clock, so we decided to come. And you're awake, so that's OK.'

'Yeah,' Johnny said, sitting back. 'Sorry, I just didn't want you to drive off without me, if I didn't come out quick enough.'

'Storm is your horse, Johnny. How could we go without you?' Ella's granny said. 'We would just have waited, that's all.'

The journey to Kiltermon was the slowest journey Johnny had ever been on. He spent a lot of the time looking over into the front at the speedometer just to see whether it would go over sixty kilometres per hour. It never did. But Ella and her granny had brought lots of food with them, almost as if they were heading off for a week's holiday, and that helped the time pass.

'What if we're late, Granny?' Ella asked. 'What if we get there when they're closing and then it's too late?'

'Ella, they close at four or five and it's half seven in the morning now and we're already on the motorway. It should only be an hour or so from here.'

'If you drove at normal speed,' muttered Johnny, just loud enough for her to hear.

'Normal speed is twice what I'm driving and I'm not going to do that, Johnny. We'll get there, don't worry.'

Ella turned around to look at Johnny and raised her eyebrows. 'It's hard not to worry, Granny, because Johnny says you can't trust them, they just do what they want. They could be tricking us, you know.'

'I know. But I believe them. They've given us this chance to come down here and see if the tracks match. Why would they do that if it was just a trick?'

'Johnny says why can't they just check the tracks themselves, why do they need us to do it? They could just email the pictures down and check and then tell us we can get him back.'

Her granny didn't answer for a while, and Ella saw her hands grip the steering wheel just a little tighter. Then she spoke.

'That's true. Yes, that is true, I hadn't thought of that. I suppose I was just so relieved to get the chance that I didn't think straight. Then Mrs Dalton said she would come down, so I thought that would do, but last night I got an email from her and she said she can't.'

'You see, Granny, already they're going back on what they said,' Ella said, looking at Johnny.

Her granny shook her head. 'I'm sure it'll be all right. She said in the email that the pound is to give us the horse if the tracks match. I've printed it out to show the pound people. She is quite clear about that. Johnny?'

'Yes.'

'Was there ever any other time where you came down with your dad to fetch a horse and the horse was gone?'

'We came down to fetch Magic, but we didn't have all the money and they said we couldn't pay it off, we had to have every last cent. So we drove back with an empty box.'

'Well, that's not going to happen here. We're going to give them that letter I have from the council, Mrs Dalton's email, and they'll let us in and we'll compare the tyre tracks, and they'll be the same, I'm sure of that, and then we'll get Storm back.'

'Maybe,' Johnny said. 'I'll only believe it when I see him.'

At that point Ella's granny turned off the motorway. 'Sorry, just need to make a stop,' she said as she pulled into the petrol station. 'I won't be long.'

Once she had stepped out of the car and was walking towards the shop, Ella turned to Johnny.

'We have to do something. Because now if we go there and they say the tracks aren't the same, then we'll just have to leave and then ...'

Johnny frowned. 'I know. Maybe when your granny goes in to talk to them and show them the pictures and everything then we'll head round the back or wherever they keep them and we'll find him.'

'But how do we stop Granny seeing?'

'I was there before and there's this office thing. That's where she'll go in, and we can say we'll wait outside. She won't mind that.'

Ella thought for a moment. 'She won't mind it, but will she believe us?'

'You know her. What d'you think?'

'Maybe. If you say it. If I say it, she'll know it's not true. She can see when I'm making something up.'

Johnny looked out of the window. Ella's granny was approaching the car.

'OK, I'll say it.'

As they drove off Ella's granny said, 'What I don't understand is why they'd go into a closed field and take him in the first place. Aren't they only supposed to take horses that are out on the roads?'

'Yeah,' Johnny said, 'but they get paid money for every horse, that's why. The council pays them, so the more horses they get, the more money.'

Ella's granny shook her head. 'I don't know. It's all wrong.

The pound can't be doing things like that – it's against the law. Are you sure, Johnny?'

'Yeah, I'm sure. You ask the council how much they have to pay the pound, it's hundreds, even thousands.'

'That's like stealing, then?' Ella said.

'It can't be the pound that does it,' Ella's granny said. 'What would they be wanting with the money?'

'I dunno. Maybe it's not the actual pound. Maybe it's some robbers that are working for them? But they'll make up some excuse. They're allowed to take horses when they're on the roads and stuff, so that's what they say, that the horses were on the roads.'

'Can't we report them to the guards, then, Granny?'

'No. I don't think there's any point. Anyway we will get him back. They just have to admit they made a mistake taking him in the first place.'

Ella couldn't see Johnny's thoughts and didn't expect to, but she stole a glance over at her granny. She didn't stay looking for very long because right at the top of the swirling thoughts was little May patting a very large horse on his nose. It looked like Giant but Ella couldn't be absolutely sure because thoughts were never exactly like photographs. She turned to look at Johnny and he was curled up in the corner of the back seat, his arms folded over his stomach, his eyes closed. Not asleep, she was sure about that, but he didn't open them. She stared ahead at the road, willing her granny to speed up, willing it all to be all right. She couldn't bear the thought of a journey back with the horsebox empty.

Time is up

At half past nine exactly they pulled up outside the gates.

'We're here,' Ella's granny said, as Johnny and Ella sat up straight, peering out of the window.

The fences were high and strong and the gate was very firmly locked.

Ella's granny got out. 'Wait here,' she said. 'There's a bell there. I'll go and get them to let us in.'

'I feel sick,' Johnny said once she had climbed out of the car.

'Me too.'

They watched in silence as Ella's granny waited. Eventually a man came out of the building and walked towards the gate. They opened the windows so they could hear.

'Good morning,' she said, handing him the letter through the bars. 'We need to come in here to check something.'

She waited while he read the letter, shaking his head as he did so.

'The transport that picks up the horses isn't ours, you

know that? It's a sub-contractor. And they have three vehicles. Only one of them is here now.'

'Well, can we come in and see that one, then?'

He shrugged. 'I suppose you're here now, you may as well. I'll open the gates.'

When she got back to the car and re-started the engine she turned to the two of them.

'Now, I just want this to go well for Storm, that's all. Even if someone says something really, really stupid or irritating or wrong, both of you keep your mouths closed.'

They looked at one another, both knowing that what lay ahead of them had nothing to do with talking, and nodded.

They rolled in and parked in front of the low grey building. They stood next to Ella's granny while she waited for the man to reach them after closing the gate.

'What are they doing here?' he asked.

'They're with me,' she said, offering no further explanation.

'Follow me.'

They followed as he walked around the side of the building and went through a further gate into a car park. In amongst the normal cars was a jeep, parked off to one side, a large metal trailer attached to it.

He pointed to it and shrugged. 'Take a look. It's nothing to me either way – we don't pick up the horses. Those trailers belong to the other lads.'

She took the pictures out of her bag and they walked towards the jeep. She crouched down and held up the picture next to the back tyre. Ella and Johnny peered over her shoulder,

'Looks the same to me,' she said.

'Exactly the same, Granny, the identical same,' Ella said. 'No-one could say anything different, ever, not even –'

'Shhhh. Have you forgotten what I asked you?'

Ella shook her head.

'Johnny, is this the kind of trailer they use?'

He nodded.

'Mister?' she called, towards the man who had been standing to one side. 'As far as we can see these are the same tyres. Would you like to look?'

'I can look, but how many of these jeeps are in the country? Thousands, what makes this one so special?' He walked towards them and bent down, glancing between the picture in her hand and the tyres. 'Yeah, they look the same. Now what?'

'Now we can get the horse back and we'll be on our way. The council said we could take him if it could be shown that there was a mistake made in picking up the horse in the first place. He was taken from a field that was rented to the owner of the horse. You do know that?'

'So they say. Which horse is it, anyway, and how long has it been here? You know we have a five-day limit.'

'He's black,' Johnny blurted out. 'You picked him up five days ago in Carrigcapall in Delaney's field. He's 14.2 hands.'

He frowned. 'Black?'

All three of them said 'Yes' at the same time.

He shook his head. 'Not sure about that. Could be his time was up. I'll go and check if he's still here. I'm not sure he is. He might have been dealt with. He's a gelding?'

'A stallion. He's chipped,' Ella's granny said, 'to John Joyce. He's here, they told us he's here.'

For the first time Ella heard a note of desperation in her granny's voice.

'Come with me,' he said. 'We'll go inside and look.' He started walking towards the low grey building.

Ella looked at Johnny.

'I think I'll wait outside,' he said, 'I don't want to go in. Can Ella stay with me?'

Her granny looked first at Johnny, then at Ella, her eyes narrowed. 'OK. But just wait here; we won't be long.'

Ella and Johnny stood absolutely still as they watched the two of them walk through the wooden doors. 'D'you think we're too late?' Ella whispered. 'You know, if they counted the night they took him as a whole day, even if the day was only one hour long? She never told me the answer to that question.'

'I don't know, Ella, but it doesn't matter now, we just have to see if he's there, that's all,' Johnny said. 'Let's go.'

He started running around to the back of the building, Ella close behind him.

'I can smell hay,' he said. 'They must be close.'

They reached a low wall and beyond it Ella could see another building, its walls rough concrete and its roof corrugated. Johnny jumped up onto the wall.

'Come on,' he said, 'we've got no time.'

Ella jumped up after him and over the wall. At the end of the building there was a huge sliding door. It was closed. Johnny grabbed hold of the handle and started pulling. Eventually it began to creak open. A loud, raw sound. Ella looked back, everyone must have heard that. The door opened just enough for them to squeeze through and they found themselves standing in a dark shed, partitioned off into what looked like stalls. The only bit of light came from the gap in the sliding door.

Johnny started whistling, a long low whistle, and then they heard it. A soft welcoming snicker of a sound.

'It's him,' Johnny shouted, not caring now who heard them. 'It's Storm.'

They both ran towards the stall and there he was, his head held upwards and his ears pricked forward.

Johnny pulled back the bolt on the stall door and flung it open.

'He's still got his head collar on,' he said. 'I'm bringing him out.'

As he reached up to lead Storm out, they heard a shout.

'Hey, you! What the hell are you doing in here?'

Ella jumped as a man appeared out of the shadows.

'I asked you what you're doing here. Let go of the bloody horse,' he said as he came closer and saw Johnny holding onto Storm's head collar.

'I won't. He's my horse. I'm taking him home,' Johnny said, sounding braver than he felt.

The man laughed. 'You are, are you? You break into private property and think you can come and steal the horses?' He pushed past Ella and walked into the stall. 'Let go, I said. Otherwise I'm calling the guards.'

It all happened so fast that Ella couldn't remember the order of things when she was asked later, but what she heard was a yell from the man in the blue overalls as he jumped to one side, and what she saw was Johnny leading Storm at a fast pace out of the stall and down the long corridor towards the sliding door.

'Come on,' he yelled. 'Run, Ella!'

Without further thought she started running after them, pursued by the shouting man. Once they got out into the yard, Johnny stopped. The man had disappeared but a loud ringing had started deep within the shed.

'They put the alarm on. Your granny will hear that and the other man will come out,' Johnny said, panting between words.

And within seconds that's exactly what happened.

'Ella, Johnny, what are you *thinking*?' Ella's granny shouted. 'I didn't know where you were.'

Neither of them replied.

She turned to the two men who were behind her. 'This is the horse I was telling you about,' she said to the older man, 'and you said you didn't think he was here.'

He shook his head. 'I said I wasn't sure, we have fifteen horses in at the moment. How can I be expected to remember every single one?'

She shook her head and turned back to the children. Johnny was holding onto Storm's head collar with both hands, a stubborn set to his mouth. Ella, who was standing a little away from them with her hands by her sides, had tears rolling down her cheeks.

'You can call the bloody guards,' Johnny said. 'I don't care. He's my horse. I'm taking him home.'

The younger man moved towards him. 'We'll see how much you don't care when the guards arrive.'

'Granny,' Ella shouted. 'Stop him! He'll do something to Johnny.'

'Sir,' her granny said, putting a restraining hand on the man's arm, 'I'd suggest you stop right there. We're here with a letter from the council and we're going to take this horse back. You can phone the woman who signed the letter if you don't believe me. The boy's father is his rightful owner. We will forgive you your error in thinking the horse was already gone, but we will not forgive you if you do anything to harm either the boy or the horse.'

The man stopped, uncertain, and looked across at the older man who shook his head. Sullenly he took a step back.

'Ella,' Johnny said, 'come and hold Storm and I'll open the box.'

'No,' her granny said quickly. 'Ella, you can't hold him – I'll open the box.'

'Granny, I know Storm. He won't do anything to me. I want to hold him. I'll be careful.'

Her granny breathed in but was saved from answering by a loud whinny from inside the shed. It persisted and got louder, more insistent.

She frowned. 'Is there a horse hurt inside?' she said, turning to the older man.

'It's probably the little coloured lad. He was in the stall next to this one.'

Ella looked at her granny and without a word she ran back inside the shed. The whinnying grew louder and she approached the stall next to the one where they'd found Storm. She peered over the stall door. Inside was a small black and white pony, no bigger than a large dog, trotting round and round the stall whinnying. He was wet with sweat.

'Granny,' Ella shouted, 'I think he's upset because Storm's gone. Come and look. Or he's sick or something.'

Her granny was already right behind her.

'Whose horse is this?' she said to the older man who had followed them in.

'No-one's claimed it, and its five days are up. Today.'

'Granny!' Ella said as she realised what he was saying. 'Granny, we can't leave him here.'

She saw the tears bright in her granny's eyes. 'Can we take him?' she said quietly to the man.

'You can take him, but it'll cost you.'

Her granny frowned. 'How much?'

'You can come into the office and we'll work it out. There's paperwork to be done for both of them. You can't just waltz out of here with whichever horses take your fancy.'

'Ella, stay here with him. I won't be long. And be careful.'

Ella turned and waited till her granny had gone back

towards the office. Then she slowly pulled back the bolt and opened the door. The little pony stopped and looked at her, his eyes bright, his breathing heavy.

'It's OK,' Ella said quietly. 'I'm not going to hurt you. We're going to take you home.' A lead rope was hanging on a hook next to the door and she reached for it and slowly approached the tiny creature. 'Don't worry,' she said. 'Soon you'll be fine, we've got lots of carrots at home and a huge field and grass and everything, you'll be fine.'

The pony stood completely still as Ella leaned forward and clipped the lead rope onto his head collar.

She breathed in and, holding the rope firmly, she led him out of the stall and down through the centre aisle of the shed, a huge grin on her face as she stepped outside.

Storm's ears pricked up as he saw them approaching and he snickered softly.

The little pony trotted up to Storm, pulling Ella along behind him, and stretched his head up to touch noses with him.

Ella's fears from earlier washed away as she watched them, scarcely able to believe that both of them were actually going to come home with them.

Suddenly she heard her granny's voice from the open doorway.

'Ella.'

'I know, Granny,' she said quickly. 'I was being careful but I didn't want to leave him there and Storm loves him and I've told him we're going to bring him home with us and now he'll be all right because of all the carrots and the grass and everything and I'm sorry I didn't listen to you but sometimes you just have to do something because otherwise it won't get done and then everything will go wrong … and he is coming home with us isn't he because otherwise I would have been lying to him?'

Her granny looked at her and nodded, then turned to Johnny. 'You'll lead Storm into the box first. I've opened it, then when he's tied in I want you to come back and bring the little one up.'

'But …'

'But nothing, Ella. Johnny has far more experience than you and I don't want anything to go wrong.'

Ella could see there was no point in arguing about this so she kept quiet and stood to one side while Johnny led both horses in. Once they were safely tied up in the box, with the hay net hung between them, her granny closed up the back and clipped it shut.

A Small Herd

'You can ride in the front on the way back if you want,' Ella said to Johnny. 'I'll get in the back.'

'Ah, no.' He shrugged. 'We'll both stay in the back. It's closer to the box in case anything happens.'

'If something happens?' Ella said. 'Like … what if the box gets undone and then it just goes down the motorway with Storm and the little one inside and then it crashes into the cars or the floor falls out underneath them and their feet are dragging on the road or we go too fast and then the box turns over … anything could happen, Granny … they're probably scared themselves in there just thinking about it.'

'Slow down, Ella,' her granny said. 'It's a strong box and do you really think I'm going to drive too fast? Really? Now, both of you get in, I don't mind who sits where but I'd like to get out of here as quickly as possible before anyone changes their mind. And I'm quite sure that Storm and his small friend feel the same.'

Johnny and Ella both jumped into the back seat, almost before she'd finished speaking, and they set off. They looked at each other, scarcely daring to believe they were going back home with a full box.

We did it,' Johnny said. 'We have him.'

Ella nodded. 'And we have his friend. Imagine that! Storm and – we'll give him a name. Maybe we can call him Smartie, you know, because he's so small and because he's clever. He called us.'

Johnny stared at her. 'Whatever. It doesn't matter what his name is, he's not going to get killed with that bolt gun thing.'

'Johnny,' Ella's granny said from the front, 'I don't want to hear about that now. I can't bear thinking about it.'

They both fell silent. Neither of them particularly wanted to think about it either.

After a while they dozed off in the back, leaving Ella's granny in a contented silence as she drove slowly and carefully home.

'Johnny,' she said, as they neared the motorway turn-off for Carrigcapall. 'Where are we going to offload Storm?'

There was no answer for a while, even though she could see in her rear-view mirror that he was now wide awake.

'Johnny?'

'I'm thinking,' he said quietly.

Eventually he said, 'I don't want to leave him back in Delaney's field tonight. I'm even scared to put him in there ever again.'

'Granny?' Ella said.

'Petal, I know what you are going to say, but –'

'But, Granny, you saw how upset Smartie was when Storm went away. We can't separate them.'

'Well, it depends what you think, Johnny.'

'What I think about what? I don't know what she was going to say. How do *you* know?'

'Hard to explain, Johnny.' Her granny looked at Ella through the rear-view mirror and smiled. Ella's eyes widened as the truth that she had long suspected hit her. They were the same, the very same, she and her granny.

'So what were you going to say?' Johnny said, a little impatient.

'Well, we could put Storm and Smartie in our field for the meantime until you decide where you're going to keep Storm. Just for the month until you decide what to do.'

Johnny looked back at the box. 'I s'pose we could. Until I find somewhere close to my place. As long as I can come and ride him every day while he's there.'

'Of course, Johnny, and it's only for now, so that he's safe.'

Ella sat back in her seat, unable to stop smiling. Storm and his little pet pony were actually going to be in the field at home. Temporarily, but still.

'It doesn't mean you can have Storm,' Johnny said, seeing her grin.

'I know, I know, I know. I'd never take him Johnny, that's mad.'

He shrugged. 'I'm just saying he can stay there till we sort out some place for him to be.'

That was good enough for Ella.

'And it's lucky they're both boys because then we can keep them together and they'll have company but Storm won't be trying ... you know ... to mate with him.'

'That's true, Ella,' her granny said, trying not to laugh, 'good thinking. Because company is so important for horses, you know that, they're much happier in a herd. Even if it's a small one.'

Dreaming of Tadhg

After the horses had been let into the field, the water for the troughs switched on and Johnny dropped back home, Ella and her granny sat down in the kitchen for a cup of tea before bed.

'So, Granny,' Ella said.

'Yes?'

'We did a good thing today, didn't we?'

'Of course we did. I wasn't one hundred per cent delighted with you and Johnny at the pound.' Ella's granny looked at her and raised her eyebrows. 'But –'

'But it all worked out,' Ella said quickly, 'and no-one got hurt and it didn't all end in tears and now Storm and Smartie are safe. So, that thing doesn't really matter.'

'That's one way of looking at it.'

'Granny,' Ella said, scrabbling around for a diversion, 'Smartie is so small that I won't be able to ride him but I will be able to do everything else. You know, groom him, feed him, pet him, without you being scared.'

Her granny smiled. 'You will, and it's a good way for

you to get used to horses. And he seems quite quiet, for a miniature. He went into the box easily enough, didn't he?'

Ella nodded.

'But the other thing is that if Storm goes back to Johnny's place, if his dad finds a place for him, then Smartie will be by himself here and you think it's cruel for a horse to be by himself and then maybe –'

'Then maybe we can look at getting him a companion that's a little bigger. We could look at getting one from My Lovely Horse Rescue perhaps?'

'Yes! That's what I was going to say. Exactly,' Ella said. 'My exact words.'

'I know, petal,' her granny said. 'I could see.'

Ella laughed uneasily, still not quite accustomed to the fact that her gift was shared in this way.

'So, what am I going to say next?' she said, putting a brave face on it.

'You are going to ask me, again, about staying down here because after all I'm too old to look after the dogs and the horses and I need company.'

Ella sat completely still, saying nothing for a few seconds.

'And if I was going to say that what would your answer be?' she said, half under her breath, 'Because it's not only all those things – it's if a horse doesn't get enough exercise then it gets fat and lame and unhealthy so if we did have another pony it would be too small for you to ride so I would have to be here, wouldn't I?'

'What I would say is one step at a time, petal. I'm going to talk to your mum and dad tonight and I am going to ask you to not ask me any more questions. If you want, you can have a small amount of extra screen time tonight and look on the My Lovely Horse Rescue site to see if there are any suitable cobs. Don't contact them because we don't know yet if this is definite, but you can look. Half an hour, then you go to sleep. OK, petal?'

Ella needed no further invitation. And, as her granny probably realised, she already knew which horses were up for adoption, as she'd spent many hours previously browsing the Adopt a Horse or Pony section of the website. Sparky, Henry, Bono, James, Bessie, Nicola, Tadhg and Little Jimbo were all names imprinted on her heart. The only problem she'd have would be in choosing between them. Tadhg was the one, though, who entered her dreams that night, trotting towards her to munch a sugar cube balanced on her outstretched hand.

The next morning she was up before her granny and tiptoed quietly past her bedroom and downstairs. Once there, she unlocked the back door and ran out to the field. Storm and Smartie were grazing peacefully in the far corner. They both looked up when she called but then lowered their heads to carry on munching contentedly. Ella stood there for a while, her heart filled to the brim with contentment, until she heard her granny shouting for her. She waved to the two of them and then turned and ran back inside to the kitchen.

'They're all right this morning,' she said to her granny. 'They're eating. And I found one. A perfect one. His name is Tadhg. They are all perfect, but he's the one for me because he came into my dream last night. He's black and white like Smartie and – well, I suppose, if we decide … Did you speak to Mum and Dad last night?'

'I did. I came up to tell you but you were fast asleep. They've both agreed that for the moment you can stay with me.'

'Really?' Ella said. 'Even Mum said that?'

Her granny nodded.

'Well, then I can see her on weekends sometimes, she might even like to come down and visit, and Dad might come back soon. Did he say he would? Did he say anything about that?' she said.

'Yes, petal, he did,' her granny said, her own joy a spark of light above her head, 'He did. He's finishing a contract this month and then he'll come home. So he'll stay here with us while he looks for work.'

'You promise?' Ella said, all thoughts of the horses flying out of her head. 'He said that? So by the end of July? In time for my birthday? Granny, you sure?'

'I am, petal. I'm sure.'

Ella sat down on the wooden chair and rubbed her tears away. 'I thought he was never coming back, Granny,' she said in a small voice. 'I thought that.'

Her granny leaned over and hugged her hard. 'He was always coming back, petal, always. He's going to call you later and you can hear it directly from him.'

Just then they heard a loud knock at the door and Ella jumped up, in her confusion imagining it was her dad arriving. It wasn't. It was Johnny standing at the door, holding a bucket of nuts and a lead rope.

Just a Small Rumble of Happiness

'I've come to see Storm,' he said. 'Mikey doesn't believe me that we got him back so he came with me but he's back there,' he said, pointing behind him.

Ella couldn't see anyone. 'Where?'

'He's hiding behind the gate post. Mikey!' he shouted. 'Come on.'

Ella watched as a boy, slightly smaller than her and Johnny, emerged slowly from behind the gate post and started walking towards them, looking this way and that as if he didn't care much about anything.

'Hi, Mikey,' she said, as he came closer.

'Well,' he said, tilting his head to one side just like Johnny did.

'We can go this way – they're out the back.'

When they reached the gate of the field, Johnny started whistling and shaking the bucket of nuts. Storm lifted his head up immediately and started trotting towards them, closely followed by Smartie, who had to canter to keep up.

Johnny turned to Mikey. 'Now?'

Mikey grinned. 'OK. But who's that small yoke?'

'He was in the pound as well.' Johnny turned to Ella. 'My da said your granny told him that someone handed him in because they couldn't look after him any more. She also told the pound that she wasn't going to pay the fee for him because they owed us one for taking Storm out of a field he was allowed in.'

Ella laughed. 'That sounds like my granny all right.'

Mikey, getting over his initial shyness, said, 'It wouldn't be the first time and it won't be the last.'

He leaned down to stroke Smartie on his soft nose. 'He looks like Blackie, doesn't he Johnny, except he's a boy. He won't grow any more, he's fully up.'

'Granny says he's a miniature Shetland,' Ella said, 'so we can't ride him, we're all too big, but he's good for keeping Storm company – and me.'

She turned as she heard footsteps. 'That's my granny,' she said to Mikey. 'She's the one drove us down.'

'Yeah, I know. I saw her by our place yesterday.'

'She looks cross,' Johnny said as she came closer.

Ella looked and saw nothing but happiness floating above her granny's head. 'No, she's not. She's happy.'

He shook his head. 'You're weird, you and your granny, the way you know things.'

'I was only guessing,' she said quickly. 'She just looks cross because her eyes are closed against the sun.' She didn't like Johnny thinking she was weird. Ella had never told anyone about her secret and she wasn't about to start now by telling him.

'I found my old grooming kit,' her granny said as she reached them, smiling at Mikey, 'so if the three of you want to get their manes combed, they're in a bit of a mess after their stay in the pound, then use this old stuff.'

She placed a bag down on the ground for them and as she turned to go she said, 'And Ella, be –'

'I know, Granny,' Ella said before she could stop herself. 'I will be.'

Johnny looked at Mikey. 'You see what I mean?'

As if joining in the conversation, Storm rested his head on Johnny's shoulder and whinnied.

Ella felt the sound travel right through her like a small rumble of happiness.

About the Author

Paula Leyden was born in Kenya and lived for many years in Zambia and later in South Africa. She now lives with her family and quite a lot of animals – many of them horses – on a farm just outside Kilkenny city in Ireland.

Her first book for children, *The Butterfly Heart*, set in her beloved Zambia, won the Éilís Dillon Award for a first novel for children by an Irish or Irish-resident author. Its sequel, *The Sleeping Baobab Tree*, won a Children's Books Ireland Judges' Special Award. *Keepsake* is her first novel set in Ireland.

Visit her website: https://thebutterflyheart.net

Acknowledgements

As always, mega-thanks to Tom and all our lovely offspring. And to the rest of our family and extended family – you know who you are. Thank you for the input, the comments and the encouragement. I'm happy to be a part of all of you. Was going to put all the names in but got to forty and stopped.

Many thanks to Siobhán Parkinson for suggesting to me that I might write a book about horses and she might publish it. And I did and she has, with patience and grace. Thanks too to the rest of the crew at Little Island and beyond – Gráinne Clear, Conor Hackett and the cover artist, Olivia Golden.

I also want to thank Bernard Power from the Kilkenny Traveller Community Movement for his insights and openness. You'll go far, Bernie. And thanks to the extended Carthy family in Kilkenny for opening their doors to me and making me feel welcome. Special thanks to all the children at the homework club in Wetlands, and to Micky Flynn who runs this homework club. You do a mighty job. And to Michael Pyke for all the work you do in Kilkenny.

I started this book while I was part of the Crabapples writers' group – thank you to all of you for your help and guidance on it.

And thanks too to (the real) Orla Mackey and Lyn Venables for reading and commenting, and to neighbours and friends for being great neighbours and friends.

And, last but not least, thank you to the children (and adults) who read my books; they mean very little without you.

The Kilkenny Traveller Community Movement is part of the Irish Traveller Movement and further information on this can be found on their website: http://itmtrav.ie/

My Lovely Horse Rescue can be contacted through their Facebook page: https://www.facebook.com/MyLovelyHorseRescue/ or through their website: https://www.mylovelyhorserescue.com/

And I can be contacted through my own website: https://thebutterflyheart.net/